KILLING WAS OUT OF THE QUESTION

One push, Ghysla thought again; then as quickly thrust the dreadful idea away. There was another answer. There *had* to be.

Then it came to her. Something that would salve her conscience—but still allow her to go through with her scheme. She could not kill Sivorne, yet keeping her a living prisoner seemed equally impossible. But there was a middle way, a way that lay between life and death, and to one who remembered the old magics from the time before the humans came, that way was still open. Sivorne wouldn't be harmed; indeed, she'd have no knowledge of her fate, for she would be in a sleep that could endure without hurt for centuries if need be. Ghysla smiled. She would take Sivorne away to her cave in the peaks by Kelda's Horns, and there she would lay the sleep upon her. The old sleep. The great sleep. The Sleep of Stone.

THE SLEEP OF STONE

LOUISE COOPER

A BYRON PREISS BOOK

DAW BOOKS, INC.
DONALD A. WOLLHEIM, FOUNDER

375 Hudson Street, New York, NY 10014

**ELIZABETH R. WOLLHEIM
SHEILA E. GILBERT
PUBLISHERS**

First DAW Printing, January 1993.

1 2 3 4 5 6 7 8 9 0

DAW TRADEMARK REGISTERED
U.S. PAT OFF AND FOREIGN COUNTRIES
—MARCA REGISTRADA,
HECHO EN U.S.A.

PRINTED IN THE U.S.A.

To the memory of my father,
Erle Antell
—simply, with love

OVERTURE

She was, the old man thought, such a lovely girl. Even though her clothes were of rough-dyed homespun and her honey-blonde hair tied into a practical braid, as with all the peasant girls of the district, her fresh complexion and sky-blue eyes—and, above all, her sweet and shy smile—set her somehow apart from the rest.

He had been sitting on a sunny ledge some way above the cave when the young couple came into view, scrambling breathlessly up the steep path. For a moment he felt a flicker of resentment; he had wanted to be alone up here in the mountains' quiet summer serenity, and the arrival of strangers was, he felt, an intrusion. But then the feeling mellowed as he reminded himself that they had as much right as he to be here. Over the years this lonely spot had become a special trysting place for so many young lovers; he had no especial claim. And so he had watched as they drew nearer. They were unaware of his presence above them and he had intended to slip away unseen when they entered the grotto, as they surely would. But when he saw the girl more clearly, that intention was forgotten, for she reminded him suddenly of someone else, someone he had once known. Old recollections stirred in his mind; but his memory was a poor and unreliable thing these days, and for the moment he couldn't quite put a name to that other face that shimmered, briefly, like a ghost in his thoughts. What he did know though, and know for certain, was that the young man by her side, sturdy and red-haired and grinning with pride in her, was a lucky young man indeed.

He continued to watch them as, hand in hand, they made their way across the scree and rough rocks towards the grotto. A streamlet, cascading down in a small waterfall from the cliff face above, sang a counterpoint to the low murmur of their voices as they reached the arching cave entrance. The girl was carrying a posy of flowers; at the entrance she hesitated for a few moments, then crouched down to place them beside the waterfall. She looked for all the world like a worshipper making a humble offering at the shrine of some elemental goddess—which perhaps, the old man thought, was not so far from the truth. Then together the couple stepped over the threshold and into the cave. More moments passed—then the girl exhaled a soft breath, and the old man smiled a private smile, for he knew what she had seen and though he couldn't see her face it wasn't hard for him to imagine her expression. Surprise, awe, even perhaps a touch of reverence at this first glimpse of something old beyond her comprehension and steeped in a mystery whose origins were long lost in the past.

For perhaps five minutes there was silence then but for the wind's secretive whispering. The young lovers were in the cave now, but no echoes of their voices drifted out. At last the old man rose from his place and, moving stiffly and with the aid of a polished stick with carved bone handle, began to make his way slowly down the small, twisting gully to the lower ledge and the grotto.

They emerged as he reached the foot of the path. Chagrin registered on their faces as they saw him; they clearly hadn't expected to encounter anyone else here—least of all, he thought with wry amusement, some bearded ancient whose trysting days were long past. But then the young man recovered his composure, touched a hand respectfully to his forelock and said, "Good day to you, Grandfather."

The old man was both surprised and pleased. Courtesy in the young—including the use of the old, polite title given to elders—was a rare thing nowadays, and any last trace of resentment he might have felt toward them vanished. He smiled gently. "Good day to *you*, my friends." He gestured toward the cave. "Does the grotto please you?"

The young man nodded eagerly, and the girl, who still clung tightly to his hand, said, "This is

9

our first visit here. It's ..." she struggled to find words. "So beautiful. So ... *strange*."

"Yes." The old man's smile became more poignant. "Yes, indeed it is. And did you find what you were looking for?"

Puzzlement crept into the young man's eyes. "What we were looking for? I don't understand."

"Ah. Then you don't know the old myth? It used to be said of this place that all who came here and ventured into the cave would find what they were seeking. A cryptic saying, to be sure, and its meaning has never been known. Perhaps it simply refers to the fact that it has always had such an attraction for young couples such as yourselves."

The girl's cheeks took on a delicate blush and she squeezed her lover's fingers. "We were betrothed yesterday," she confided in a voice brimming with shy happiness. "So we thought that we should come here, to ... well, to pay our respects."

"And to bring you good luck for the future." The old man nodded. "Very wise, very wise; my warm felicitations to you both."

There was a pause. Then, hesitantly, the young man spoke again.

"Pardon me, Grandfather, but do you know this place well?"

"Oh, yes," the old man told him. "I often come here when the weather is fine, to rest my bones in the sun and contemplate old times. I know it very well indeed."

"Then perhaps ..." He seemed about to falter, but the girl pressed his hand again, encouraging him, and he regained his courage. "Perhaps you know the real legend of the grotto?"

A gentle inclining of the grey head. "Perhaps. Though it's an old, old tale now and almost entirely forgotten."

"They say," the girl put in shyly, "that once, long ago, a very great love story was enacted here; and that's why ... why ..." she blushed crimson, and the old man chuckled.

"Why it's now the favorite haunt of so many young lovers, and said to bring them luck? Ah ..." A love story? he thought. Well, perhaps in its own strange way it had been that. But how many people could remember the legend now? Time changed all things beyond recognition.

He said: "I do know the tale, though I must be among the last of those who do, for it was old even in your grandparents' time."

The girl glanced back over her shoulder to the grotto. Deep shadow shrouded the interior, but in the dark a faint, nacreous gleam was just visible.

"Please, Grandfather, will you tell it to us?" she asked.

The young man shook her gently by the shoulder. "Hush, Linni! The Grandfather has better things to do than talk to us!"

"Oh, but I haven't." The old man's gaze moved from one to the other of them. So often the young folk had no time for their elders, and to find a pair so eager to pass the time with him and listen to his stories was refreshing indeed. He smiled at them again. "Indeed, if you're willing to indulge a sentimental ancient, then I'm willing to talk for as many hours as the day grants us!"

They looked eagerly at each other. "They say it's a sad tale," the young man said.

"Well, yes; though some might think otherwise." The old man moved toward the cave, his stick tapping on the rock, and stopped at the entrance. Spray from the cascading waterfall touched his face like tiny needles. He paused briefly, then stepped inside.

Yes, there it was. He hadn't looked on it for many years now, but it was still exactly as he remembered it. A strange rock formation, a stalagmite composed of many different minerals and shimmering with its own rainbow of patterns and colors. Time and the elements had eroded it but it still maintained an echo of what must have been its original shape; a shape that rang faint, disturbing bells in his imagination.

The young couple had followed him into the cave, and he saw from their faces that they, too, felt that peculiar and unidentifiable sense of familiarity. He reached out as though to touch the stalagmite, then thought better of it and instead turned the movement into a simple gesture toward it.

"You see this strange and fantastical stone," he said, his voice echoing hollowly in the grotto's confined space. "It could almost have been carved by a human hand, couldn't it?"

The girl drew an astonished breath. "*Was* it?"

"No." The old man shook his head slowly. "No, it was not. But this piece of rock, this— memorial, you might say—lies at the very heart of my tale." Turning, he gently ushered them before him, back out into the dazzling sunlight. He couldn't tell the story here in the cave. Somehow it wouldn't be right and proper.

"What happened here," he said, "began many hundreds of years ago, or so the legend runs." Stiffly he eased himself down onto a small ledge, settling with his back against the rock wall. "Did you know that another race of beings used to live among these mountains, before humans came to the western coast?"

They had sat down at his feet; wide-eyed, they shook their heads. He smiled. "It's true. Man is a relative newcomer in these parts; before his time there were others, a far older people whose lives spanned not mere decades, but centuries. They looked a little like us, but only a little, for they were elemental creatures; mortal in their way, but with something of the beast and something of the bird and a little of something that neither you nor I could put a name to in their souls. The human races, when they saw them in their true form, dubbed them gremlins; but they were mistaken in that, just as they were mistaken in believing that they were, by nature, evil. They were not evil: they were simply *different*." He looked at them for a long moment. "Would you kill a spider, which does you no harm, simply because it has eight legs and you have two? Or," seeing the girl flinch faintly and guessing—rightly—that she was afraid of spiders, "the cat who keeps mice from your threshold, because she has whiskers and a tail and you do not? No, I see you wouldn't do such a cruel thing; because you accept them for what they are. And if only our ancestors had accepted the old race of creatures for what they were, then perhaps this legend would never have come into being. But that was not so: And therefore you and I sit here today in the sun, many hundreds of years later, and I have a story to tell where otherwise there would have been nothing."

The girl's expression was very quiet now, almost grave as she listened intently. The young man too was thoughtful; then he reached suddenly to a sack that he carried slung over one shoulder, and drew out firstly a leather bottle and then a clean linen bundle.

"Grandfather," he said, "we have victuals and ale here." He unwrapped the bundle, revealing a hunk of cheese and a good, newly baked loaf, still warm from the oven. The aroma of it made the old man's nostrils tingle deliciously. "Will you share it with us while you tell the tale?"

"An offering? I'm touched by your kindness, young man; and I thank you. Yes." He reached out to take the proffered beer and uncorked the bottle. "Yes, I'll eat and drink with you gladly. Give me a piece of that fine bread and a sliver of cheese. And now you shall hear the *true* story of this grotto. The story of Ghysla . . ."

CHAPTER I

A storm was brewing out over the sea, devouring the fierce sunset, when an axle on the first of the carts sheared in two. The party—some eight horsemen as well as the pair of four-in-hand wagons—came to a chaotic halt, and the mountain pass rang with irritable voices as men gathered round the stricken vehicle to see what could be done.

Dusk came swiftly this late in the year, and the heavy clouds massing from the west deepened the twilight to a dour, artificial gloom. A few of the party's more nervous members glanced occasionally at the lowering twin crags known as Kelda's Horns and made religious signs in the air or touched their fingers to talismans around their necks. Legends of things better unsaid and unseen were rife in this wild land, and though no one *truly* believed in such tales, or so they told themselves, neither were they willing to risk attracting the evil eye from some denizen of the mountains.

But the signs they made and the prayers they

muttered were merely symbols, not true magic. They had no power to affect Ghryszmyxychtys, as she crouched behind a rocky outcrop a hundred feet above the pass and gazed down upon the scene with burgeoning interest.

Ghryszmyxychtys, in the old tongue of her kind, meant *the little dark one*. But she had lost count of the years that had passed since anyone had spoken that name aloud. Another race with another tongue ruled this land now, and her own ancient language was forgotten. Only she remembered, for she was the last of her kind, and even she had bowed to the new order of things and learned to translate her name into the simpler speech of humans. She was not Ghryszmyxychtys, not now. Her new name was Ghysla.

An arm thin as a blackthorn twig was looped lightly over the rocks' surface, and the hand with its long nails, like a bird's claws, clenched with excitement as Ghysla peered into the gathering dark. Her night vision was as acute as any cat's or owl's; indeed, her vast, tawny eyes might have been taken for those of an owl, had they not been framed in a sharp, delicate face that was almost—if not quite—human. Long, ragged hair hung over her back in a matted mass, tangling with the membranous wings which grew from her shoulder blades. Her feet, also clawed, gripped her stone perch, and she was so motionless that to the casual eye she might have been a part of the mountainside, a piece of granite

17

scoured by the elements into a nightmarishly half-familiar form.

But Ghysla was acutely, painfully alive. She could feel her heart thumping in its cage of sharp ribs, and her huge, slit-pupiled gaze was fixed unmovingly on the wagon—and especially on the golden-haired girl, surrounded by clucking older women, who sat within it.

So, she thought in her own language, which was not the language of humans, she has come. And the blood in her veins seemed to slow to a crawl as a mixture of misery and fury overtook her.

There was renewed shouting from below, and a string of oaths hastily silenced as the men saw what Ghysla had already realized. The wagon couldn't continue. To mend the axle would take hours, and with night and the storm coming together they didn't have the luxury of time. One of the horsemen dismounted and several of the men went into a huddle, talking urgently. Straining her ears but still unable to hear anything of their conversation, Ghysla moved cautiously from her hiding place, sidling a little way down the slope in the hope of gaining a better vantage. She stopped only when she saw that torches were being lit, and her lips drew back from the needlelike teeth in a frustrated hiss. Fire was anathema to her; she feared it above almost anything else, and even without that fear she dared not allow its light to fall on her and expose her to the humans below. So she froze, trying to pretend that the guttering flames didn't make her stomach turn over with sick fright, and stared again at the scene.

Someone was talking to the golden-haired girl, and a hand reached up to help her down from the cart. Ghysla's mind flamed like the torches with a jealousy that almost took her breath away as for the first time she saw the girl clearly, and realized how lovely she was. Then, carried on a capricious gust of wind that snatched the words across the pass and to her avid ears, she heard a name, a destination, and knew without any doubt who the beautiful young woman must be.

In the town of Caris, five miles on, the local lord whose family had given the town its name lived in a great house that stood proud and aloof above the harbor; and rumor had been rife for months now that Anyr, only son of the house of Caris, was soon to marry. Ghysla had heard the rumor during one of the frequent visits she paid to the harbor during the twilight hours between day and night. She loved the town; its life and bustle drew her like a moth to a candle's flame, and she had shape-changing skills which enabled her to disguise her appearance well enough to pass for just another fishwife or dockside ragamuffin. Lurking amid the shadows of the wharves, or flitting between the lit windows of the taverns with their smoke and shouts and unfamiliar, fascinating smells, she had picked up a snippet of talk here, a whispered word there, which said that an eastern landowner's flaxen-haired daughter was coming from inland to be pledged to their own lord's son, and that she would bring with her a dowry which would ensure the house of Caris's prosperity for many years. Ghysla had told herself that the rumors were doubtless as wild as all the other gossip so beloved of the town's tabbies, and when nothing seemed to come of the tales—no gathering excitement, no obvious preparing for a celebration—she was, for a while, almost convinced. But deep down in her heart she couldn't shake off the dull, miserable ache of unformed dread, and on this stormy evening, as she gazed down from her high vantage point into the gloomy valley, that dread swelled into terrible, soul-tearing certainty. For these strangers had the smell of the east about them, and the girl in their midst had hair the color of a spring sunrise. Who else could she be but the landowner's daughter, the intended, the bride come to claim Anyr as her own?

And the girl who would take away the man that Ghysla loved to the depths of her soul.

She hadn't meant to fall in love with Anyr. She'd tried to tell herself at first that it was a foolish and futile emotion, for surely the gulf between their worlds was far too great ever to be bridged. He was human, a lord's son; she was . . . well, she was Ghysla. Neither woman nor beast nor bird, but a little of all those things, a chimera, a gremlin. How could Anyr ever feel for her as she did for him? He would only have to

20

look once upon her face, her *true* face, and he would turn from her in revulsion. Or—worse by far—he would laugh at her presumption and mock her and drive her away. But that knowledge hadn't been enough to deter Ghysla. Indeed, all the wisdom in the world hadn't been enough, since that day by Uilla Water three years ago, when she had set eyes on him for the first time. And it was on that day that Ghysla's miracle had begun. . . .

She was lying sprawled at full length on a rock that jutted out into the sea at the foot of the shelving cliff plateau which humans called Cann's Steps. The sun had only just risen and the cliff's long shadow reached out from behind her, sheltering her in its gloom. She was reaching down into the green-black foaming water, trying to tickle and catch the fish that surged shoreward on the incoming tide, when her animal-sharp ears caught the faint vibration, carried through the rock, of someone approaching. As swift and as wary as a fish herself, Ghysla sprang to her feet and darted to the shelter of a small cave. The intruder was probably an angler risen from his bed early to catch the best of the tide, and she cursed softly under her breath, knowing that she must find some stratagem to get away unnoticed, or risk being trapped uncomfortably in the cave for the entire day. Her shape-shifting powers seemed to provide the only answer. She had the ability to change her appearance in the eyes of mortals and deceive them into seeing her in whatever form she visualized for herself. The changes were hard to maintain and took a great toll of her energy, but necessity was necessity; and Ghysla had just decided that she would take on the likeness of a seal—which no fisherman would ever harm—and brave the unpleasant prospect of having to splutter her way through the cold salt water and away round the point out of sight, when a footfall above her set a shower of loose shale rattling down the slope, and he appeared.

Ghysla had never seen a god, but for one glorious moment she was convinced that the figure who stepped into her view, with his hair as warm and brown as the sweet summer earth and his eyes the color of the sea with the sun lighting on it, must have come down on an eagle's wings from those high and magical realms. The fancy fled, of course, when she saw that he wasn't dressed in the light of suns and moons and stars, as a god would surely have been, but in old hide trousers, frayed and patched in places, and an open-necked shirt of good but well-worn homespun. His feet were bare and in one wind-browned hand he carried a rod and line, while a bag, bait tin, and water bottle were slung over his left shoulder. He was tall, lightly built, with a kind and handsome face. He was perhaps twenty years old. And Ghysla, peering from her hideaway and unable to tear her gaze from him, fell instantly and hopelessly in love.

She didn't leave the cave as she had planned to do. All thoughts of changing her form and escaping from the bay vanished from her mind as she continued to gaze at the beautiful stranger, and she resolved that however long he might remain here, be it an hour or a year, she, too, would not leave. So she stayed crouching, watching, avidly drinking in everything she could see of him, everything she could learn of him. She watched as he baited and set his line and sat down on the rock to await the first bite. She listened to the songs he sang to himself, trying to memorize every word of the verses, every nuance of the melodies. When he drank, she too made the motions of drinking, and licked imaginary drops from her chin with her long tongue. She watched the way that the sun, climbing higher, reaching the meridian and then starting to slip down again toward the western horizon and the sea, played on his face, on his hair, on his hands. She silently and delightedly applauded each fish he caught—there were nine—and when suddenly he began to pack up his rod and she realized that the day was almost done, she clenched her fists until they hurt as desolation overcame her. He was leaving. Her young god, her beautiful young man, was going away, back to his home, back among his own kind. She was about to lose him, and he didn't even know of her existence.

Ghysla had tried to tell herself that to follow him was both foolish and dangerous, but her heart refused to listen to reason, and as he began to climb back up the steep rock shelf she crept out from the cave and stood watching to see which direction he would take when he reached the clifftop. He turned north, toward the harbor and the town, and as soon as he was out of sight she took a deep breath, shut her eyes and concentrated with all the strength of her will. Then she dropped to all fours and, bounding, scrabbling, sliding, set off in pursuit.

If Anyr had chanced to look back over his shoulder as he walked home that night, he might have seen a deer or a dog or a small, shaggy pony following cautiously some thirty paces behind him. Ghysla was so excited, so nervous and so filled with her thoughts of him that she couldn't maintain any one image for more than a minute at a time. Sometimes she trotted on small, slotted hooves that made no sound in the heather; sometimes she padded on soft paws with her tail waving hopefully and her tongue lolling. Once, to her horror, she glanced down at herself and saw that she had the nacreously scaled legs of a dragon and that her feet had turned to talons, and in shock she flicked back to her own form and lay flat in the heather, panting like a hound and not daring to move until she could bring her shape-shifting back under control.

Eventually they reached the town. The young man didn't stop there, didn't turn in to any of the fishermen's houses, but walked the length of the street and across the harbor, then began to stride up the steep road that led away toward the

24

far cliffs. That road led only to the house of Caris, home of the overlord, and, looking now to any casual observer like just another old crone of a fishwife hurrying home after a day's gutting and gossiping, Ghysla followed him up the long hill to the big wooden gates. There, hidden in shadow, she heard the gate guard greet him as "master" and the tiny flame of hope which had been lurking stubbornly deep down within her died. He wasn't a servant, as she had begun to believe. She should have known it, despite his rough and worn clothes, for his face was too fine and his bearing too confident. He was no servant, but an aristocrat. He was the son of Caris, heir to this house, to its lands, to the town itself. And that placed him as far above her as the moon was above a blade of grass.

The gates closed behind him, and Ghysla slunk away in the deepening dusk. Somewhere in the back of her mind a small voice of reason was trying to tell her that his rank made no difference to the dashing of her hopes, for, master or servant, he was human and therefore beyond her reach. No human could ever love her, the small voice insisted, for to human eyes she was a travesty and a monstrosity. Some might pity her; a few—though she'd never dared to put it to the test—might be willing to be her friend, but even to the kindest of them she would always be a thing and not a person. But, floundering as she was in the riptide of this new emotion, Ghysla paid no heed to the inner voice. Today she had learned the meaning of love, and she was caught as surely as a spider caught a fly.

That night, Ghysla returned to her eyrie high up in the crags. Although she was tired—like humans, she needed sleep—even the idea of sleeping was beyond her now. Visions of the handsome young lord filled her mind, and though she berated herself for a fool she couldn't forget about him. Nor, she resolved, could she bear to go on with her life as though nothing had happened. She must see him again. She *must*.

Alone in the cave which had been her home for more years than she could count, Ghysla sat and began to form a plan. At first, as her ideas took shape, she was haunted by crowding doubts; but after a while the doubts began to fade under the tide of her eagerness, until finally they were submerged and lost altogether. She could do this. She *would* do this. No matter how much time and how much courage it might take, she would find a way to make herself known to the young lord. Not in her true shape, not yet. But in other forms; forms which would please his eyes and make him look kindly on her. Kindness, Ghysla told herself as her heart began to beat more quickly, was not so very far removed from love. If she was careful, and patient, and diligent, who could say that the one might not become the other in time, and so fulfill the dream that had awoken so suddenly and powerfully in her lonely heart?

CHAPTER II

Before the first glimmer of dawn painted the eastern horizon the next morning, Ghysla left her hideaway and hurried down to Caris. From long experience she knew all the best places where gossip could be overheard: the market square at the heart of the town, the narrow, cobbled streets where wives chattered on each other's doorsteps, the harbor itself where human activity was almost ceaseless. And today it seemed that luck was smiling on her, for harborside she found a great gaggle of women waiting for the fishing fleet to come home with a new catch. The fishwives of Caris could be relied on to know everything that went on in and about the town, and to talk ceaselessly of it; and so, hidden in shadows, unnoticed, Ghysla watched and listened and committed to memory all that she heard.

She learned a good deal that day and during the days that followed. She learned not only Anyr's name but also his habits; where he liked to go, what he liked to do, the times of the day when he was most likely to venture alone from the great house on the clifftop. "The young master went riding yesterday," the women said; or: "Young lord Anyr came through the town early this morning. Going fishing, no doubt; he'll not be home until dusk." Ghysla was excited to discover that Anyr spent a great deal of time alone, content, it seemed, with his own company. He had little interest in the more rambunctious sports of hunting and racing and fighting that so many young men of his station enjoyed, preferring to go for long rides across the inland moors, or to walk the clifftops from where he could watch the sea and the birds that nested on the high promontories. Often he went fishing at Cann's Steps or one of the many other little bays and inlets along the coast—and it was at one of these bays that Ghysla finally plucked up the courage to make her first move.

It was a good day for fishing. Rain in the night had calmed the sea to a gentle swell, and now there was a fine, drizzly mist in the air, encouraging the fish to rise. And an hour after dawn, Anyr made his way down the cliff path to settle himself for a day's pleasant work.

Ghysla saw him from her perch among the stones of an old cairn on the cliff, and her thin little face broke into a smile. Rising from her crouched position she ran along the clifftop, keeping low lest he should look up and glimpse her, until she came to the adjoining inlet. There was no path here, but the steep climb was no obstacle to Ghysla and within minutes she had reached the water's edge below.

A short while later, a new sound amid the splash and slap of the waves against his ledge made Anyr raise his head. He had already landed one fine sea bass and was hoping for a second to bite at his line when he heard something that didn't fit with the rhythm of the tide. Looking up, he saw a sleek, dark shape moving by a cluster of rocks some twenty feet from shore. Suddenly a larger wave rose over the rocks, and the shape launched itself into the green wall of water, twisting and diving gracefully, until the wave broke and it vanished in a welter of curdling foam. Then, as the undertow swept back, a brindled and bewhiskered head broke the surface, bobbing only ten feet now from the ledge where Anyr sat, and he heard the sweet mournful, whistling call of the seal above the sea's roar.

A smile of delight curved Anyr's lips, and, as he had learned to do as a child, he whistled an answer to the seal's cry. The creature's great brown eyes blinked slowly, its body shivered as though with pleasure—and, so swiftly that his eyes could barely follow, it dived deep into the water and was gone.

Anyr looked for it through the rest of the day, but he didn't see it again. He was disappointed, for he loved all animals; and besides, to be befriended by a seal was said to bring great good luck. What he didn't know—couldn't have known—was that, as he whiled the rest of the day away on the rock ledge with the baited fishing line at his side, his seal hadn't left the bay but was still nearby; nearer than he could have imagined. Ghysla had fled to a smaller cove just around the headland, and there she shed her disguise and sat on a high rock above the water, hugging herself as she relived and savored the wonderful moment when he had called to her, and wishing with all her heart that she had had the courage to stay.

But with time, courage came. At first she dared do no more than watch Anyr from a distance, which she did at every opportunity. Then, secretly, she began to follow him; never in her true form—that, she thought, she would never dare to do—but in the guises of the beasts and birds which he loved. She was a skilled shape-shifter, and her ingenuity in disguising herself was limited only by her imagination. When Anyr went riding across the moors on his favorite sorrel mare, then she was a vixen or a stoat scurrying invisibly in his wake. When he went fishing she was a seal again, bobbing in the water and watching him through the blurring green swell of the tide. Once—gloriously—she was an eagle, hovering high above him when he exercised the mare along the clifftop, though this venture was short-lived because she didn't have the stamina to maintain both the power of flight and her shape-changing for long. In a multitude of ways and a multitude of guises her one-sided courtship of the lord's son continued, and her love for

him, far from loosening its first soul-wrenching
grip, grew deeper and stronger.

Anyr, of course, knew nothing of her feelings—and for a long time it could, in truth, be
said that he didn't even know of her existence,
for Ghysla took the greatest care never to let her
disguises slip for one moment when she was in
range of his sight. He might smile at the fallow
doe which unexpectedly trotted across his path,
he might listen with pleasure and admiration to
the song of the bird that perched in a tree above
his head, but he saw nothing and knew nothing
of Ghysla as she truly was. At first Ghysla was
content with that, for although she was unable
to show herself to Anyr, reach out to him and
say to him, *I am here, and I love you*, she could
at least pretend that such a thing might one day
happen, and keep the tiny flame of hope alive.
But as the months went by and the seasons
changed, she began to yearn for something more.
To adore Anyr from afar wasn't enough. The tiny
flame wanted to become a blazing fire—and at
last she plucked up the courage to take a greater
and braver step than she had ever dared to do
before.

She chose the guise of the brindled seal in
which to carry out her plan, for of all the creatures whose forms she adopted Anyr seemed
fondest of the lonely sea-mammal. Again Anyr
sat fishing on his favorite ledge, and again, as had
happened so many times before, he saw the familiar grey head rise above the waves. He whis-

tled to it as he always did, wishing that it would lose his fear of him and come closer. If only men and animals could communicate, he thought—if only he could make the seal understand that he would do it no harm but wanted only to be its friend. . . .

Then his body tensed as he saw that, instead of keeping its distance as it usually did, the seal was in fact drifting toward the ledge. No; not drifting, for it wasn't simply allowing the tide to carry it shoreward. It was *swimming* toward him, cautiously but deliberately approaching. Anyr held his breath, his fishing line forgotten, and watched with wide, eager eyes. He didn't dare to utter a sound for fear of frightening the seal away, but in his mind he silently and fervently encouraged it. *Come, pretty one; please come closer. Come to me; I mean you no harm!*

Ghysla couldn't see into his thoughts, but she saw his smile and the light in the eyes, and knew something of what he was feeling. Her heart seemed to turn over within her as a giddying mixture of joy and terror swamped her, and she almost lost her courage altogether and, with a flick of her tail, dived back under the water and away. But something—perhaps that unquenchable little flame of her hopes—stopped her, and for a few moments she stayed rocking gently on the swell, her big dark eyes regarding Anyr solemnly and uncertainly.

Slowly, Anyr dropped to one knee on the rock and extended a hand. "Pretty one . . . pretty seal. . ."

He had never spoken to her before, and a great shudder ran the length of Ghysla's disguised body. "I won't hurt you. Please, come to me. Come to me and be my friend."

His smile became a soft chuckle of delight as, hesitantly at first but then with growing confidence, the seal swam toward him. He could almost believe that it had understood his words. Nearer now, nearer; and then suddenly the sleek body touched the rock wall below him, and the creature raised its head from the water to push its muzzle against his outstretched fingers.

For as long as she should live—and that might be many centuries yet, for her race did not age in the same way that humans did—Ghysla knew she would treasure that moment as the happiest and most thrilling that she had ever known. She could barely feel the touch of Anyr's hand through the seal's thick hide and dense fur, but the effect on her was as great as though she'd been struck by a bolt of lightning and left unscathed but shuddering with shock. She uttered a sound that was halfway between a moan and a cat's purr, and Anyr laughed again.

"There, pretty one! Do you like to be stroked? What a fine coat you have; like rough silk. Here, now." Leaning back, he patted the rock ledge at his side. "It's a fine day. Come and bask with me, little seal. Lie beside me and enjoy the sun, and I'll see if I can't catch enough fish to sate us both!"

Ghysla needed no second invitation. By now

her fear and shyness were things of the past, and quickly she swam to where the rocks sloped in a way that allowed her to haul herself awkwardly out of the sea. She flopped along the ledge to join Anyr, and settled herself beside him, her body quivering and her eyes aglow with happiness. Anyr, not knowing the real truth, was delighted, and wondered anew at the seal's seeming ability to understand him. And so they stayed while the day wore on, the young lord with his newfound companion at his side. He stroked Ghysla's head and laughed delightedly at her purring response. He fed her more than half of the fish he caught—she didn't really like fish, but she ate them with pleasure because they were his gifts to her. And he talked to her, as he might have talked to an old and dear friend. Ghysla drank in every word he said as though it were the sweetest wine, and as she listened she marveled over and over again at the miracle which fortune had bestowed on her. She was happier, she believed, than any creature ever born, for Anyr was beside her, and Anyr had touched her, and Anyr was her beloved and now her friend. The world was perfect, and Ghysla's life was complete.

That beautiful, magical day was only the first of many such days for Ghysla. The seasons turned on their way; summer into autumn, autumn into winter, winter into the new promise of spring; and the bond between the little shape-changer and her adored Anyr grew ever stronger.

Anyr himself didn't understand what truly lay behind the strange and wonderful things that happened during that year and the two which followed it. He thought—and how could he have known otherwise?—that somehow, by means that were a mystery to him, not only the shy seal but all the other wild creatures of the coast and moors and woodlands had suddenly learned to trust him. First there was the young doe, an exquisite creature with great brown eyes and legs as slender as the stem of a flower. He had glimpsed her before, at a distance, but now each time he came to the woods she sought him out, running to meet him and eagerly eating from his hand while he stroked her small head. Then the hare, nervous and lop-eared, with its nose constantly twitching for danger, which hopped to sit at his side in the long grass at the edge of some cornheavy field. The songbird that fluttered down from the trees to alight on his shoulder and carol to him. The vixen with her handsome red-brown mask and thick tail swishing the long grass to express her pleasure at his caress. They loved him, all of them, and Anyr in his turn loved them. They were his dearest friends.

As for Ghysla, she truly believed that nothing would ever threaten her newfound happiness. Seal or deer, hare or bird or fox, whatever guise she chose, she was Anyr's own beloved. She knew it because he told her so, as he stroked her fur or feathers, or fed her morsels and tidbits, or spoke sweet, loving words to her. She was his, and he loved her. So surely he, in a subtle way, belonged to her in his turn. With that knowledge safe and secure like a precious gem held close to her heart, she had been utterly, blissfully content.

Until tonight . . .

The sky was growing darker, the storm clouds almost overhead now and the setting sun no more than a thin, fire-red line on the horizon. Ghysla could smell the rain coming and see it moving in grey columns out over the sea; far away in the distance lightning flickered briefly, though too far away for the thunder to be heard. She stared down at the wagons, at the torches, at the girl with the golden hair, and wished that the heavens might open and bring a great flood flashing down through the valley to sweep them away to the ocean and drown them in its deepest chasms. But the old gods, who might have granted such a wish, were dead and gone, and the heavens didn't answer her fervent prayer. Instead the men were helping the golden-haired girl onto a horse; the others, too, were finding mounts and they were about to abandon the stricken cart to ride on to Caris. The procession formed up, the escorts' torches—how Ghysla *hated* those fearful flames—guttering as the wind gusted suddenly and violently from the southwest, and with a shout of command from the leader they moved off into the gathering dark.

For a long time after they had disappeared,

Ghysla crouched motionless among the rocks. The rain began but she cared nothing for the fact that it was soaking her, turning her wild hair to rats' tails and running in rivulets from her skin. Only when lightning erupted almost overhead and the first huge bellow of thunder shook the crags did she at last rise from her perch.

The girl with the golden hair had come to take Anyr from her. That was all she knew; and the knowledge burned like a fever within her. She had come, and on the day that Anyr took her hand in marriage, Ghysla's heart would die and turn to dust. She had tried so hard to convince herself that the rumors were untrue, that there was to be no lovely eastern bride and no wedding, and that the bond between herself and Anyr would not be forced apart and shattered; but now she could no longer keep up the pretense. The truth had confronted her in all its stark cruelty, and she couldn't deny it any longer.

Then in the midst of her misery, self-pity gave way to a new emotion. She'd been thinking only of herself—but what of Anyr? How must *he* be feeling on this terrible night? He didn't love this bright-haired human girl. He *couldn't* love her, for he already had another love, a truer love. What had his own people done to him, what had they said and what had they threatened, to force him into this loveless match? Anyr's heart didn't belong to the eastern girl; it belonged to her, to Ghysla. She knew it, for he had told her so.

Suddenly Ghysla began to tremble as though with a palsy. This wedding must not take place. It must not be. Anyr might be trapped in the web others had spun and powerless to stop it, but she was not; and his salvation—indeed, the salvation of them both—lay in her hands alone. She would not let the wedding happen. And she believed she knew a way to stop it.

She looked up at the sky, and as if in answer to her thoughts another flash of lightning blasted brilliantly through the peaks. The elements were her friends; the wind would carry her and the lightning and thunder would give her the power she needed. She could do it. For Anyr she could do *anything*, if only she willed it.

The wings at her back rose like fragile sails. She spread them, testing their strength, then launched herself up and out from the crag and flew, buffeted on the rising gale and with the rain streaming in her hair, away toward Caris.

CHAPTER III

"Raerche, my old friend!" Aronin, lord of Caris, crossed the great hall of his house with his arms outspread in greeting. "Welcome! Welcome to my home!" He clasped the hands of the thin-faced, patrician man who led the small party, then turned to embrace the man's plump and pretty wife. "And my dear Maiv—gods preserve us all, what a night this is! Come, come to the fire and get warm!"

More kisses and exclamations were exchanged as the guests were hurried to where a huge blaze roared in a grate the size of a cave. Servants ran to take sodden cloaks and ease off wet riding boots, and stewards hastened in with wine and mead and beer and trays of bread and sweet cakes. And a new voice, eager, joyful, almost reverent, said: "Sivorne . . ."

There was a sudden lull in the noise as everyone turned to look. Anyr had entered the hall behind his father, and now he stood a few steps from the hearth, gazing at the golden-haired girl. Slowly he held out his hands, and the flush which the ride had brought to Sivorne's cheeks deepened while her lips smiled and her eyes shone through rain-speckled lashes.

"Anyr." Her voice was no more than a whisper, but it carried a wealth of emotion. Anyr's hands covered hers and held them tightly, and shyly she let him kiss her cheek. The servants looked on, smiling; Aronin beamed and Sivorne's parents exchanged a happy glance. The two families were old friends; Anyr and Sivorne had known each other since they were children, and from their very first meeting it had been clear to all concerned that, one day, they would be far more to each other than youthful playmates. They'd seen little of each other in recent years, but distance hadn't dimmed the bond between them, and their parents were content in the knowledge that, as well as being a sound pragmatic alliance, this marriage between the son and daughter of their two houses would also be a love match.

Anyr and Sivorne had much to say to each other, but the sweetest of those words would be kept for a more private moment. For the present, there was a good deal else to occupy everyone's minds. Aronin had ordered a feast in his guests' honor, and before the celebrating began there was baggage to be transported to the visitors' bedchambers, hot baths to be enjoyed and fresh clothes to be changed into after the rigors of the journey. In the house's kitchens, a flurry of activity was in progress as the preparation of the feast vied with the heating of water for the baths. A young servant-girl, braving the storm to refill two large ewers from the well, only briefly noticed the bedraggled cat that huddled just outside the door in the pouring rain. She felt a quick stab of pity for it, as she would for any creature without shelter on such a foul night, but she hadn't the time to translate pity into help. When she returned the cat was gone, so she quickly forgot its plight. And no one noticed the little shadow that, having slipped through the door that the servant girl had left ajar, crept across the kitchen between a forest of hurrying feet and, following instinct and its nose, sneaked through the house and up flights of winding stairs, finally to arrive at a pleasantly furnished bedchamber with a fire in the grate and a woman's elegant gown laid out on the bed. There was no one in the room, and the cat's shape flowed and re-formed into that of Ghysla. She backed away from the fire with a sharp hiss, and from the safety of the farthest corner by the window surveyed the room. This was the one, there was no doubt of it. *Her* room. And later tonight *she* would climb the stairs and slip under the warm blankets and go to sleep. Ghysla fingered the heavy curtains at her back. There was a deep alcove in the window, a fine hiding place, and she wriggled behind the curtain and settled herself. All she had to do now was wait.

* * *

Lord Aronin was a contented man when he retired to his bed that night. The feast had been a thoroughgoing success and now his guests were comfortably settled and sleeping soundly. Even the storm had abated at last, rampaging away inland and leaving a clear, starry sky over the sea and above Caris. That, he thought, was a good omen; and a better portent still had been the light of happiness that had shone in his son's eyes when Sivorne had set foot over his threshold. A love match, there was no doubt of it. Aronin was glad, for his own marriage had been blessed with love and he had wanted nothing less for Anyr. His only regret was that his own wife hadn't lived to share in the joy of this occasion, and when everyone else had left the great hall and he was sure he was alone, he paused before extinguishing the last candles and went to stand before the portrait, all he had left of her now, that hung on the wall beside the west window.

"Did you enjoy the evening as much as I?" He spoke tenderly, reaching out to touch the face in the painting as he had done every night for eleven years now, and paused for a moment as though waiting for an answer to his question. No answer came—he'd long ago given up the fancy that she might speak to him across the years and across the gulf of death—but Aronin smiled as in his imagination he heard her voice. "I think it went well," he said. "And I truly believe that they'll be happy together; as happy as we were." He stepped back a pace and made a bow. "Goodnight, my dear."

He pinched out the last candle. The flame died with a tiny hissing sound, and Lord Aronin made his way to bed.

The screams from the west wing brought Anyr flailing out of a pleasant dream, and for a moment, in the throes of shock, he couldn't imagine where he was or what the source of the terrible sounds might be. Then reality crashed in to drive out the stupor of sleep.

"*Sivorne!*" He'd never heard her scream but somehow he knew instinctively that it was her voice, and he fell out of bed, stumbling across the darkened room toward the door. He stubbed his toe, cursed at the pain, reached the latch and flung the door open in time to meet Raerche in the corridor outside.

"Anyr!" Sivorne's father had a short-bladed sword in his hand; his eyes were wide with fear and fury together. "Which way? Which way is her room?"

Of course; he didn't yet know the layout of the house ... Anyr grabbed him by the arm and they began to run along the corridor. Maiv, Sivorne's mother, appeared at the door of her own chamber, her hair unbound and a robe wrapped about her; she called out anxiously but the two men ran on, not heeding her. Sivorne's room lay in one of the house's turrets, and as they reached the short flight of spiral stairs that led up to it, Aronin and two servants came pounding along the passage from the opposite direction.

"Blood of gods, what's happening?" Aronin was out of breath, and his words were barely audible above the terrible cries coming from the top of the stairs. Anyr made to go first but Raerche pushed past him and took the stairs two at a time.

"Sivorne!" He hammered on the bedchamber door. "*Sivorne!*"

Anyr caught up with him and tried the latch. It lifted, and they ran into the room together.

Sivorne was sitting up in the bed. The room was dark, but enough starlight shone in at the window to etch her like a pale ghost. She had covered her face with both hands and was rocking violently back and forth, her screams now punctuated by huge, rattling sobs as she struggled for breath.

"Sivorne!" Raerche and Anyr ran to her side together. "My sweet child, what is it? What's happened to you?"

Sivorne sucked air into her lungs with a terrible sound, reaching out blindly to clutch at their arms. "Here!" she gasped. "In—in the room, it was in the *room*—"

There was a renewed flurry in the doorway as Sivorne's mother arrived, followed by her tire-woman. She ran to her daughter and embraced her, and Aronin ordered a lamp to be lit. As the darkness was banished by soft yellow light Anyr saw that the curtains were half open. Thinking that this might answer the mystery he went to investigate, but found the window shut fast and the bolt still in place. No assailant could have left that way—and besides there was nothing outside but a lethal two-hundred-foot drop over the cliff edge. Puzzled, he pulled the curtains together again. He didn't see the shadow that shrank back into the deep window alcove as his hands gripped the heavy fabric, nor the glimmer of huge eyes staring at him as Ghysla felt his breath on her face; nor did he notice when the curtain continued to tremble for some seconds after he released it. His only concern was for Sivorne.

With the lamplight and her loved ones to reassure her, Sivorne was eventually calmed, and at last she told her story. She had woken, she said, to feel another presence in the room. For a moment she had thought that it must be morning and a servant had come to relight her fire and bring her hot water for washing, but then she realized that it was still pitch dark. Nervously, she asked who was there—and someone or something sighed close by her ear. She cried out in fright, turning her head, and then she saw it.

"I don't know what it was!" she said, shaking her head in distress while her mother hugged her and Anyr held tightly to both her hands. "It was like—like an owl, and yet like something else, too; a fox or a—a—" She caught her breath as words failed her. "And then ... then, the worst thing of all ... its face changed, and for one terrible moment it became *me!*"

Above her bowed head Aronin and Raerche

exchanged a troubled look. Then Raerche bent over the bed.

"My child, it must have been a bad dream." he said gently. "The rigors of our journey— you're exhausted, and the mind can conjure strange fancies at such times."

"No!" Sivorne shook her head again, so that her golden hair flew about her like a halo. "It wasn't a dream. I was *awake!*"

Maiv flicked her husband a warning glance that clearly said, *don't argue with her now*, and patted Sivorne's cheek.

"Whatever it was, my sweet, it's gone now and we are all here to take care of you." She looked up again. "I shall sit with her for the rest of the night."

"My dear, you're as tired as she is," Raerche protested.

"Perhaps, but I don't want her left alone." Maiv glanced round the room with narrowed, suspicious eyes, as though expecting something to materialize from the shadows.

Aronin spoke up. "I have a better solution. Anyr's old nurse—come to that she was my nurse, too, when I was a babe, and she still lives here in retirement. She's a wise-woman and a healer in the bargain. Let her sit with Sivorne tonight. She could have no better guardian." He turned, snapping a finger to one of the servants. "Wake Coorla, and tell her we need her here. Tell her to bring her nostrums." As the man hastened away, Aronin smiled, trying to be reassuring though his face was still pallid. "Coorla will stand no nonsense from demons, be they real or imaginary."

Raerche and Maiv were a little reluctant to agree, but finally their own weariness persuaded them that Aronin's suggestion was the best; and when the nurse arrived their doubts were assuaged. Coorla was thoroughly eccentric but also utterly capable. She treated both Anyr and Aronin as though they were still children in her charge, and her fierce authority soon encompassed both Sivorne and her parents as well. She prepared a sleeping draught for Sivorne, muttering darkly as she mixed a pinch of this herb and a few grains of that into a cup of wine, and her bright little eyes, almost lost in their surrounding wrinkles, watched intently as the potion went down. Then with no further ado she banished everyone else from the room, asking tartly how the poor child could be expected to sleep with half the household trampling like a herd of wild horses round her bed.

Anyr was the last to leave. He kissed Coorla on one leathery cheek, making her chatter and cluck at him, then took Sivorne's hands again and bent to kiss her more intimately on the lips.

"Enough, now," Coorla said sharply. "There'll be time in plenty for that when you're wed, and the child needs her sleep! Go on with you, and shut the door behind you."

On the threshold Anyr paused. "Take good

care of her, Coorla. If any harm were to befall her . . ."

Coorla snorted indignantly. "As if anything the night brings could harm a hair of her head with me to watch over her! Go to bed, boy, and stop fretting."

From behind the curtain Ghysla heard the door close and Coorla shuffle back to the bed. There were some low whisperings, answered by Sivorne in a sleepy and faintly slurred voice, and then the sounds of the old woman making herself comfortable in a chair. Silence fell, but Ghysla remained motionless. Her mind was in turmoil, for the passion she had heard in Anyr's voice as he took Sivorne in his arms and tried to comfort her had shocked her to the core. To hear him then, it was almost impossible to believe that he didn't truly love his bride, and fear crawled like spiders inside her as she wondered if she had been wrong, if she had misjudged her beloved. But no, another inner voice argued. She wasn't wrong. Anyr did *not* love Sivorne; he was simply fulfilling the duty that was expected of him, and trying to make the best of the situation into which he had been forced. His lips might say one thing; his heart knew another.

Comforted and reassured—she would not, *must* not let herself succumb to doubt—Ghysla refocused her attention on the bedchamber, invisible beyond the curtain's heavy folds. An odd noise was now intruding on the silence, and after a few moments Ghysla realized that old Coorla had begun to croon a low-pitched song; a lullaby she suspected, though she had no experience of such things for no one had ever sung to her in her cradle. Coorla's voice was gratingly off-key, and there was something about the song—the words of which seemed to be in an unfamiliar language—that disturbed Ghysla deeply. She began to shiver. Could Coorla be a witch? Was that what Lord Aronin had meant when he called her a "wise-woman"? Human sorcery frightened Ghysla, for she had no means to combat it; the power in mortals' spells and incantations was inimical to her and caused her intense pain. She huddled down under the window ledge and put her hands over her ears, trying to blot out the old woman's droning voice, and after a while, to her intense relief, the singing faded first to a mumble and finally to silence. Then, after a pause which lasted an unguessable time, Coorla began to snore.

Ghysla's hopes rose with a sharp jolt. The nurse, it seemed, wasn't quite the stern and reliable guardian that she claimed to be. Her old bones clearly didn't take kindly to being roused from rest in the middle of the night and she had fallen asleep in her chair.

Slowly, cautiously, Ghysla pulled the curtain aside until she could see a little of the bedchamber. There was Coorla beside the banked-down fire, her back to the window and her grey head nodding in rhythm to her snores. There was the bed-foot, and a spill of light from the lamp that must be standing near Sivorne's head. Ghysla nibbled nervously at her lower lip and pulled the curtain back a little farther. Ah, yes—there was Sivorne herself, still and calm beneath the blankets. And, by great good fortune, she was lying on her back so that her face was clearly visible. Maybe, Ghysla thought, the old gods were on her side tonight after all. For with Sivorne drugged and her protector oblivious, she had the chance she needed to complete her unfinished work . . .

She eased herself out from behind the curtain and silently tiptoed toward the bed. The herbal draught had done its work and Sivorne showed not the slightest reaction as Ghysla's shadow, grotesque and elongated in the lamplight, fell across her. Ghysla gazed down at the golden-haired girl. She was, indeed, *very* beautiful. That would make her own task all the harder, but no matter—it could be done, and it *would* be done.

The plan had come to her as she waited in the darkened room for Sivorne to arrive and retire to bed, and she had been so thrilled by it that she'd almost cried out aloud. Anyr had been forced to pledge himself to Sivorne, and now that the pledge had been made he couldn't gainsay it. But what if, instead of looking for a way to stop the marriage from taking place, she herself were to take Sivorne's place by Anyr's side on the day of the ceremony? What if she were, to all intents and purposes, to *become* Sivorne? Was she not a shape-changer? Anyr already knew her in a dozen different guises, so surely if she could appear to him as a seal or a deer or a bird then she could also appear to him as his own bride? No one would be able to tell the difference, and so no one—not even Anyr—would know the truth until the wedding was over and the vows had been made, and *she*, Anyr's true beloved, was his wife in Sivorne's stead. And so when Sivorne fell asleep, Ghysla had crept out of hiding to crouch over the bed and gaze silently, intently down at her, trying to memorize every detail of her face; the curve of her lips and cheek, the exact shade of her hair. She hadn't expected Sivorne to wake, and as the girl screamed she had fled in panic back to the window, struggling to force it open and fly out and away into the night. But the bolt had jammed, and instead she had been forced to conceal herself behind the curtain again, holding her breath and praying that she wouldn't be found. Now, it seemed that the window's resistance had been a blessing in another guise.

She dropped to an ungainly squatting position and drew as close to Sivorne's sleeping countenance as she dared. A faint, sweet scent emanated from the girl's skin, which was so fair and delicate that Ghysla, fascinated, longed to reach out and touch it. She had never been this close to a human before. How fine her hair was; as fine and brilliant as a cobweb with the dew shimmering on it. And her body, slender and yet smooth and rounded; no stick-thin limbs or ungainly torso or razor-boned shoulders ... envy filled

Ghysla, but she thrust it from her mind, the pupils of her great eyes widening like a cat's as she gazed into Sivorne's face as deeply and as intensely as though she were trying to drink her soul. She must learn *everything* about this golden-haired beauty, so that her deception would be perfect.

She was so enraptured, so mesmerised by her task and by the excitement that thrilled through her like a tide, that she didn't hear the sudden telltale creak of the chair by the fireplace. Concentrating with all her willpower, Ghysla was in the throes of trying to shape-shift her own face into an exact likeness of Sivorne's, when a cry of astonished outrage made her leap to her feet and spin round.

Coorla had woken. For a moment in the uncertain lamplight she hadn't been sure if what she saw was an intruder or merely a shadow cast by the room's furnishings. But as Ghysla sprang up and turned, the old woman saw her clearly— a grotesque sight, for she was in the midst of her transformation and her vast, alien eyes glared wildly from Sivorne's lovely countenance while her hair was a bizarre piebald of fine gold and coarse, matted black.

Coorla's own eyes opened wide, and with a speed and agility that belied her years she too was on her feet. "*Demon!*" she yelled, her voice shrill with fury. "Ah, *demon!*" Then she drew herself up and her eyes glazed over as she raised both arms in a dramatic gesture. "*Casha fiarch, auchinar ho an tek!"* she cried. *"Fiarch, fiarch, ranno ho, teina ho—"*

A violent pain burned through Ghysla's head as the words of Coorla's incantation seared her mind. She opened her mouth and howled, outrage and defiance vying with her fear. Oh, but the old witch's spell was *hurting* her! She had to stop it, or the pain would overwhelm her and send her screaming, reeling, groveling in agony and as helpless as a newborn babe. Goaded by panic, Ghysla didn't pause to reason: she sprang at Coorla, her wings beating wildly and giving impetus to her leap, and the old nurse's chant was cut off in a strangled squawk as bony, clawed hands clamped around her throat. Hissing now like a maddened snake, Ghysla beat her wings again and rose three feet into the air, lifting Coorla off the floor. The old woman was a dead weight and her kicking and struggling almost pulled Ghysla's arms from their sockets, but she clenched her teeth and wrenched, dragging Coorla across the room. They struck the edge of the window alcove and suddenly Ghysla's wings tangled in the curtains so that, flailing off balance, she lost her grip on Coorla's throat. The nurse fell to the floor with a heavy thump; for a few seconds she sprawled, coughing and spluttering, then she recovered her wits and began to croak her incantation again with renewed fervor. *"Fiarch, fiarch, ranno ho—"*

Ghysla cried out, and for one instant as she panicked anew and lost control, her face became

Louise Cooper

that of a squealing pig. The window—she had to
reach the window, had to get it open this time!
As the words of Coorla's spell blazed into her
brain she wrenched at the bolt—and this time
she must have gripped it in just the right way,
for it grated back and the window shot open with
a noise like a death rattle. Chill night air rushed
in, setting the curtains flapping wildly. Coorla
was still chanting, her voice gaining strength now
as she recovered from Ghysla's choking stranglehold, and with another cry Ghysla turned on her.
She couldn't bear it any more, she couldn't fight
against the power of this human spell. She had
to make the nurse *stop!*

Terror and rage combined to goad her, and she
grabbed the old woman under the arms, jerking
her off her feet again. Her wings flapped frantically; she rose, Coorla rose helplessly with her,
and in a burst of sudden maniacal strength
Ghysla heaved the old woman straight at the
open window. A flurry of arms, legs, and skirts
blurred before her vision—then Coorla hurtled
through the window and plummeted down,
down over the two-hundred-foot drop of the cliffs
to the heaving sea. Her thin, high-pitched shriek
echoed back on the wind, but Ghysla couldn't
look, couldn't bear to watch her fall. Then the
old woman's last despairing cry faded out, and
the only sound to be heard was the sea's steady,
implacable roar.

Ghysla stood very, very still as cold horror froze
her mind. In the room before her Sivorne slept

on in the glow of the soft lamplight, unaware of the struggle and its shocking outcome that had taken place only a few paces from her bedside, and the peaceful scene was horribly incongruous. At last a sound broke the silence as a choked-off sob escaped from Ghysla's throat, and she covered her face with both hands. *She hadn't meant to hurt the old woman!* She hadn't wanted to hurt *anyone.* She wasn't evil—she'd never done such a thing in her life before, never *dreamed* of doing such a thing, and remorse filled her with suffocating agony, as though she were drowning. Fear, and the desperation of her love for Anyr, had overcome all reason and she had acted wildly, madly, terribly. Now Coorla was dead, her body taken by the sea, and she, Ghysla, was her murderer.

She stood trembling by the window and, unable to face the full horror of her guilt, her mind began to search frantically to justify what she had done. Surely, she told herself, there had been no other choice open to her? Coorla's spell would have overpowered her and left her writhing in helpless agony; Lord Aronin would have been summoned and she would have been at his mercy. What would have become of her then? Punishment, imprisonment—even execution. She had had to stop Coorla. She had *had* to.

She looked at Sivorne again. Still the golden-haired girl didn't stir, and by a miracle it seemed that no one else in the house had been woken by the second rumpus from the turret bedroom.

Ghysla crept hesitantly toward the bed. Dawn wouldn't break for some hours yet. She had time to continue her work; and she yearned to continue, to complete what she had begun. Her love for Anyr was too strong for guilt and remorse to deter her.

Slowly she dropped to her knees by Sivorne's side. Cold air slid in at the still-open window, and the ceaseless sound of the sea was a muted murmuring in Ghysla's ears as she gazed down hungrily and with obsessive concentration at the girl's sleeping face.

CHAPTER IV

"It's a great embarrassment to us, of course," Aronin said, "but thankfully there was no harm done." He crossed the hall to the tall south window, from where he could gaze out over the harbor waking now to the bustle of morning, and shook his head. "I can't for the life of me imagine what could have got into Coorla that she should have betrayed our trust in such a way."

Anyr followed his father across the room and stood beside him. "Perhaps she's simply too old to be relied on, Father." He smiled fondly but a little sadly. "You know how eccentric she's become this past year or two. She's taken to disappearing for a few days at a time and then coming back as though nothing had happened. I suspect that's what happened last night. She simply took it into her head to go off again, only this time she inconvenienced us all by leaving her post in the middle of the night."

"Yes; doubtless you're right, Anyr. All the same, I'll have some sharp words to say to her when she does return. What must Raerche and

Maiv think of us? We promised that Sivorne would be guarded, and that promise was broken. We neglected our duty."

"But as you yourself said, Father, there was no harm done."

"No." Aronin's expression relaxed a little. "No, that's true." He paused. "How is Sivorne this morning?"

Anyr's smile became warmer. "I haven't yet seen her. She's closeted with her mother, but I believe they'll both join us at breakfast. Raerche tells me that she slept soundly for the rest of the night, and has suffered no ill effects from her fright."

"I'm very relieved to hear it," Aronin said. "I'm convinced it was nothing more than the rigors of the journey that upset her and gave her nightmares. And of course there are only five more days to go before the wedding—the poor child must be all of a dither with nervousness and excitement."

"I assure you, she isn't the only one!"

"I'm sure that's true! Still, it's a fine day today. You can take Sivorne out and treat her to some of our clean sea air: it'll put color in her cheeks and drive out the mind-shivers." He patted his son's arm, beaming at him. "It'll do you both good to enjoy your own company for a while, away from us musty old ones!"

Anyr returned the smile affectionately. "Perhaps she'd like to go riding. She hasn't yet seen the dappled mare that we bought as a gift for her."

"That's right, that's right. Take her through the town and let the people see and admire her. After all, she'll be their lady very soon!"

A bell sounded at that moment, summoning the household to breakfast, and with their arms companionably linked Anyr and his father left the hall. As they disappeared, a door at the opposite end creaked open a little way and a small, wild-haired figure dressed in a serving maid's plain homespun peered into the hall. Then, seeing that the two men had gone, Ghysla abruptly let her disguise slip, and her enormous, owllike eyes were wide with wonder as she stood in her own likeness on the threshold of the room.

Ghysla had crept away from Sivorne's turret long before the dawn had begun to break. She had lost her bearings three times among the house's rambling stairways and passages but at last had found her way back to the kitchen, where the scullery maids were snoring on their pallet beds, and from there to an outhouse. She was wearied to the bone by the energy she'd expended, and hadn't wanted even to think about the dreadful thing she had done to Coorla: crawling onto a pile of half-full sacks, she had fallen asleep immediately and only woke when morning came and the household began to stir. To her relief she found that sleep had cleared her mind of its confusions, and just now as she had listened to Anyr and his father talking she had for-

gotten her tiredness, forgotten her guilt about
the old nurse's fate, and resolved more deter-
minedly than ever to complete what she had set
out to do.

A careless remark of Aronin's had shocked her
to the marrow as she listened from behind the
door. Five days before the wedding was to take
place. That was all the time she had: just five
days to make herself into such a perfect twin of
Sivorne that no one would be able to tell the
difference between them. Last night she had
achieved much, but it wouldn't be anything like
enough. She must work harder. She must follow
Sivorne wherever she went, learn her every gesture, memorize each little quirk of her voice, im-
itate her laughing or weeping, merry or sad.
Nothing less than perfection would do.

She looked furtively about the hall, and suddenly her gaze lit on a pair of shoes by the heart.
Small shoes, dainty and pretty and decorated
with bows; *her* shoes, soaked by last night's
downpour and set by the fire to dry. Ghysla flung
a swift, nervous glance over her shoulder to ensure that no one was about to discover her, then
darted across the hall. Luckily the great fire had
gone out overnight, or she would never have
been able to approach the hearth; but where
flames frightened her, dead ashes did not. She
snatched up the shoes and, crouching, turned
them over and over in her hands, marveling
at their delicacy, stroking the curved heels, lifting them to her face so that she could sniff the

mingled smells of the damp wooden soles and the soft, pliable leather. These shoes were a part of Sivorne, a link with her. Delighted with her prize, Ghysla tried to slip them on to her own feet. The attempt was a miserable failure, for her clawed, splayed toes would no more fit these dainties than a rabbit would chase a fox; but when she concentrated hard, recalling what she had learned during her vigil of last night, her feet suddenly became small and white-skinned and human, and the shoes slid on as though they had been made for her.

She stood up and moved experimentally across the floor. She had never worn anything resembling shoes in her life before, and the alien feel of them, complicated by the inch-high heels that Sivorne favored, made her movements clumsy and uncertain at first. But after a few minutes' perseverance she thought that she was beginning to master the knack of walking in these strange contraptions, and the small triumph delighted her. She would keep the shoes. They would be a talisman. And five days from now she would wear them for Anyr when he took her hand in his and they spoke their nuptial vows.

Sounds impinged from the passage beyond the door; the brisk clack of footsteps accompanied by the chatter of several voices. Servants were coming, doubtless to light the fire and prepare the hall for the day, and with a start Ghysla kicked off the shoes, bent to scoop them up as a mother hen might scoop her chicks under her wing, and ran toward the far door. One quick glance told her that the coast was clear, and she scurried away through the door and down a short flight of steps that would take her, by a round-about route, back to the sculleries where she could pass unnoticed amid the general bustle of activity. Seconds later, a steward passing her on the steps saw only a quick blur of brown hair and grey skirts, and snapped a finger imperiously.

"You! Tell the cook that the master and his guests are ready for their breakfast to be served!"

Ghysla looked up; the steward had an impression of a plump, pockmarked face and a vacant expression.

" 'Es, sir," the creature muttered, and hastened on her way, leaving him none the wiser.

Sivorne plucked a late gillyflower from where it grew in the shelter of the mellow old stone wall, and turned to give it to Anyr. He took it, deliberately catching her fingers along with the green stem, and she laughed delightedly as he sniffed the petals and their peppery scent made him sneeze.

"You've pollen on your nose." She stood on tiptoe to kiss it away; then abruptly her expression grew more serious. "Oh, Anyr ... I'm so happy!"

Anyr put the flower in her hair, then took a gentle hold of her arms. "Are you, truly?"

"Yes! And today. . . ." she looked around her at the quiet, private garden, sheltered behind its substantial walls from the ravages of the sea gales, and a haven of tranquility. "Today has been wonderful. Your people are so kind—when we rode through the town I was greatly moved by their welcome."

"You are their new lady," Anyr told her, "and they already love you." One hand touched her face gently. "Though not as much as I do. That would be impossible."

She laughed, warmed by his compliment yet still just a little shy with him. They had, after all, had so very few chances to be alone together before today, and she felt that for the first time she was truly coming to know him. The knowledge kindled a flame of deep content within her, for it confirmed all her hopes, all her dreams. Anyr would be far more than a husband to her. He would be her one and only beloved, her soul-companion, the light of her life. No woman, she thought, had ever been as lucky as she was.

They walked slowly, leisurely to where an old wooden bench hugged the lee of the south wall, flanked by tall shrub borders that made a suntrap even in this late season. As they sat down, Anyr said, "And do you really like our countryside?"

Sivorne smiled radiantly. "It's beautiful. So wild and untouched, and the western air is so *clean*. In my home, we seem to be plagued constantly by east winds, and Mother says that they're unhealthy because they come from farther inland and carry all the miasms and fevers that are absent from sea air."

"The west coast is said to be the healthiest place in the world." Anyr smiled back at her, then his expression grew a little wistful. "I'm only sorry that we didn't encounter some of my friends on our ride."

"The wild animals and birds you told me of? Yes, I'm sorry, too. I'd so wanted to see them. It must be wonderful to win the friendship of such creatures and be trusted by them." Her fingers linked with his and squeezed shyly. "Perhaps they didn't come because I was there and I'm a stranger. I hope that, one day, they'll learn to look upon me as a friend, too."

"They will," Anyr said, his voice suffused with pride. "Like all the people hereabouts, they will only have to see you to love you."

She laughed with pleasure. "Dear Anyr, you're flattering me! If I didn't know better, I'd think . . ." Her voice trailed off.

"Sivorne?" Startled, Anyr saw that she was staring fixedly into one of the shrub borders and her eyes had widened as though with shock. "What is it, what's wrong?"

"I—" Sivorne put a hand to her face as color flared in her cheeks. "I thought I saw—" Her hand began to shake.

"Saw what? My love, what is it?"

"No." Abruptly Sivorne stood up, staying him as he was about to put his arms about her. "No, Anyr, it was nothing. Just a trick of the light." She shivered. "It's growing cold. Please—may we go back to the house?"

"Of course!" He began to lead her away from the bench; she seemed to want to hurry and he steadied her as in her haste she almost tripped over the hem of her gown. As they moved toward the house Anyr looked back, wondering in puzzlement what could have upset her, but he could see nothing untoward. Only the bushes and the empty bench, and the plucked gillyflower lying on the lawn where it had fallen from Sivorne's hair. Nothing else. Nothing else at all.

As the sound of the garden door closing echoed in the evening quiet, Ghysla rose from where she had frozen among the bushes. She hadn't been able to overhear any of the conversation between Anyr and Sivorne, but she knew what Sivorne had seen, and she was furious with herself for the lack of control that had enabled the girl to glimpse her, if only for a single moment. She stared hard at the house through the blue eyes that were such a close copy of Sivorne's own, and the wind from the sea blew hair like spun gold gently about her shoulders and stirred the skirt that matched Sivorne's in every detail. She knew that the image wasn't right yet, not completely right—but this incident had proved that it was close enough to have struck terror into Sivorne's heart when she had seen what she took to be her own twin gazing at her from the shrubbery. Of course Ghysla shouldn't have made the mistake of letting Sivorne see her, but she had been concentrating so intently that she'd let caution slip. No matter, she told herself; it had at least proved that her work was progressing well. And it was only one small lapse. Sivorne wouldn't connect it with the fishwife who had watched her so closely as she rode through the town, nor with the bird that had alighted on her window ledge and gazed in at her while she changed out of her riding habit into fresh clothes. She had learned a lot today, Ghysla thought with satisfaction.

Lamps were beginning to come on in the great house as the sun set over the sea. The garden was sinking into shadow with the approach of night. In the great hall Sivorne and Anyr had rejoined their families and were drinking wine together; already Sivorne was beginning to forget her strange, momentary vision. No one looked out to the garden again, and no one saw the pale-haired figure that glided like a silent ghost from the shelter of the bushes and away across the lawn, to vanish in the deepening dusk.

Preparations for the wedding of Anyr and Sivorne began in earnest the next day. Bunting and flower garlands were being put up in the town and along the harbor front, while all manner of entertainer—musicians, jugglers, poets, and more—began to rehearse their party pieces in earnest, hoping that they would be among the select few invited to perform at the nuptial revels. From early morning a seemingly endless procession of visitors toiled up the hill to the house of Caris: merchants' carts laden with foodstuffs, vintners and brewers with barrels of wine and mead and beer, and, it seemed, a representative of nearly every family which owed allegiance to Aronin, with some small gift for Anyr and his bride.

Inside the house, all was in cheerful turmoil. In Sivorne's turret room a gaggle of women including Maiv and two seamstresses from the town fussed and clucked around the bride, putting the finishing touches to her wedding gown and discussing how she should wear her hair for the great occasion. Anyr, too—though under some protest on this fine, sunny day—was suffering the attentions of the tailor and the bootmaker and the barber, while the great hall and the kitchens below rang with the sounds of activity.

As the afternoon began to wane, Sivorne at last escaped from the hectic bustle. The men were still busy, so she and her mother took a stroll through the gardens. They walked slowly around the edge of the neatly trimmed lawn, not talking but content simply to enjoy the cool air. And behind them, keeping a careful distance but anxious not to fall too far behind, went Ghysla, a shadow among the shadows as she watched Sivorne's every movement with avid eyes.

She didn't mean to let the golden-haired girl see her. Perhaps the strain of keeping up her disguises had wearied her more than she'd thought, or perhaps, as before, it was just the result of a moment's carelessness or overconfidence; but either way she was caught unawares when Sivorne suddenly stopped walking and looked back over her shoulder. Ghysla didn't have the chance to vanish into the bushes or change her appearance. For the third time Sivorne saw her—and screamed.

"Sivorne!" Shocked, Maiv spun round. "Child, what is it?"

"Look!" Sivorne pointed at the spot where Ghysla had been lurking. Maiv looked, but saw nothing, for in the split second before she turned around Ghysla had dived into the shrubbery and vanished from sight.

Sivorne clutched her mother's arm. "There was something there!" she said, her voice shrill. "I saw it, mother. I *saw* it!"

Maiv frowned uncertainly, and Ghysla, peering fearfully through the shrubbery's tangle, crouched lower and tried to make herself as small as possible. "What did you see?" Maiv demanded.

Sivorne was shaking. "A—a monstrosity! Just like the creature I saw in my room the night before last—oh, Mother, it was a kobold or a gremlin, I *know* it was!"

"Now, Sivorne, that's nonsense. What gremlins could there be here? This isn't the wild mountain land; this is Lord Aronin's own garden! My dear, it must have been a trick of the eye, perhaps a shadow—"

"No!" Sivorne shook her head wildly. "No, Mother, it was *real!* It darted away into those bushes before you could glimpse it, but it was *there!*"

"Into the bushes? Well, let's see, shall we?" Maiv gathered up her skirts and started to move purposefully toward Ghysla's hiding place. Horrified, Ghysla tried to hunker down even farther but then realized that she couldn't possibly escape detection. Maiv bore down on her; she shut her eyes, concentrated with all her might—

"Oh!" Maiv jumped back with a start as the bushes suddenly rustled, then she laughed as, with a frightened *miaow*, a large tabby cat scurried from the undergrowth and streaked away toward the house. "There!" Maiv said to Sivorne. "There is your gremlin—nothing but one of the kitchen cats."

Sivorne stared at the shrubbery. "But I saw—"

"Now, daughter," Maiv's voice became firm. "There was no gremlin, and nothing at all for you to be frightened of." She took Sivorne's arm, turned her around and started to steer her back the way they had come. "I think that the bad dream you had the other night must have affected you more than any of us realized. It's little wonder, with the arduous journey we had through those gloomy mountains and with all the excitement you've been subjected to since our arrival here." She reached up and felt Sivorne's brow. "I don't think you've taken a fever, but all the same I shall ensure that you have a quiet day tomorrow. You'll feel better for a good rest; it will calm your mind and enable you to forget these fancies."

For a moment it seemed that Sivorne might protest or argue, but she thought better of it and only nodded. Her mother shepherded her into the house, and there was no more talk of nightmares or gremlins. However, after the evening meal was over, Maiv went quietly down to the kitchens and instructed a senior servant to ensure that a good dose of sleeping-herbs was put into a hot drink and served to Sivorne in her bedchamber later that night. She swore the servant to secrecy, not wanting to worry her husband or her hosts, and went to bed content that Sivorne would suffer no more nightmares, and convinced that all would be well from now on.

Sivorne slept through the night as peacefully as a newly fed babe. And when the last servants had retired and the house was dark and silent, Ghysla crept up the turret stairs, as she had done before, and crouched at the golden-haired girl's bedside to continue diligently and tirelessly with her secret work.

CHAPTER V

Maiv had been confident that Sivorne would suffer no further troubles, but she was sadly wrong. By the time two more days had passed not only she but everyone else in the household was deeply concerned, for it was clear now that something was very amiss with the bride-to-be.

True, there had been no more nightmares, but what had taken their place was, in Maiv's view, far worse; for Sivorne had begun to suffer from hallucinations in broad daylight. It seemed that she couldn't be left alone for more than five minutes without some new vision assailing her. Walking in the gardens, sitting by the fire in the hall, even in her own room, time and again her screams of terror shocked the household, and on each occasion her story was the same—she had seen a kobold or a gremlin, and its face was a parody of her own.

On the third day they called in a physician. He was Aronin's own man and renowned for his skill, but after examining Sivorne and talking earnestly to her for some while he confessed himself defeated. There was nothing wrong with the girl; indeed, she was in the peak of health. Her mind didn't wander and he could find none of the tell-tale signs of dementia. Yet she still persisted with her story that a gremlin was dogging her every step. In his view, he said privately to Raerche and Aronin, what the child needed wasn't a physician but a witch.

Aronin didn't like resorting to witchcraft. He had always discouraged such practice among his liege-folk, for he believed that it opened the gates to too many charlatans and tricksters. But for once it seemed he had no choice, and Maiv was emphatic that the town's wise-women must be consulted. So some seven or eight of them came, and they looked at Sivorne, and they muttered together in a corner of the hall, and then they set up their braziers and their crucibles of incense, and they chanted long into the night in an effort to drive the evil miasms away. But their spells had no effect on Ghysla, for she had overheard a steward telling a maid what was afoot, and had already fled down to the harbor where the old women's sorceries couldn't affect her, and there she waited until the work was completed and the witches went away.

She was angry with herself for the clumsy mistakes that had allowed Sivorne to glimpse her on so many occasions, but at the same time she knew that she had no choice but to take the risks. Time was running out; there were only two more days now before the wedding was to take place and she *must* be perfect in the role she planned to assume. Her one consolation was the knowledge that both Aronin and Raerche still believed Sivorne was suffering from hallucinations and nothing more. They had called in the witches to pacify Maiv and not because they themselves gave any credence to the idea of a lurking gremlin and once, in her now familiar disguise of a kitchen cat, Ghysla had overheard the cook telling the head steward that the physician, on a second visit, had pronounced Sivorne's affliction to be simply acute prenuptial nerves.

Ghysla sneaked back to the house that evening, sniffing the air carefully before she entered the scullery to ensure that there was no lingering whiff of human magic in the atmosphere. All was well, and once more she melted into the general chaos of the servant's quarters. Tomorrow, a rehearsal of the wedding ceremony was to take place in the great hall. This, for Ghysla, would be the most vital phase of her preparations, for it would show her what the bride must do, and what she must say, on the day of the wedding itself. To her great relief she learned that the servants were to be allowed to watch the practice of the rite. That night, rather than go to Sivorne's room as was her custom, she crept away to one of the outhouses and allowed herself the luxury of a few hours' rest. She didn't need sleep in quite the way that humans did; an hour here, an hour there was enough to refresh her. But during the last few days she had come close to exhaustion, and she needed to replenish her strength now while she still had the chance.

Ghysla spent the night dreaming wild and glorious dreams of Anyr, and woke with the dawn to prepare herself for the day ahead. When, at midmorning, the house servants filed in to stand respectfully and eagerly at one end of the great hall, no one noticed an extra girl among the excited, whispering group of scullery-maids in the corner.

A respectful hush fell as the two noble families entered the hall, and the rehearsal began. Sivorne, dressed today in a simple wool gown and not in the finery she would wear tomorrow, looked pale and ill. There were deep shadows under her eyes and she seemed unable to concentrate. Several times she had to be prompted as to where she must stand and what she must do, and she kept looking quickly, nervously over her shoulder as though expecting to see something lurking behind her. Ghysla noticed her discomfiture and felt a twinge of guilt, but it didn't last; she was too intent on watching and listening as the wedding practice continued. There was so much to learn, so much she would have to remember, and in fact she had good reason to be thankful for Sivorne's hesitations and mistakes, for many parts of the ceremony had to be rehearsed several times over before the two families were satisfied that all would go smoothly when the proper time came.

They finished at last, and Maiv didn't allow

Sivorne to linger but hurried her away to her turret room with strict instructions to rest. The servants shuffled out of the hall and back to their duties, and Ghysla took her chance to slip away into the garden, to find a private, undisturbed spot where she could go over and over the ceremony and commit it firmly to memory. In the hall, Aronin, Raerche, and Anyr lingered, gathering together by the hearth. Anyr stared into the fire, his expression faraway and unhappy, and after a minute or so of silence Raerche cleared his throat.

"She'll be all right, Anyr. It's simply nervousness; you heard what the good physician said yesterday." He laid a hand on Anyr's shoulder and patted it sympathetically. "Once all the excitement's over, and you can settle down as man and wife, she'll be her old self again."

Anyr looked up with a pallid but grateful smile. "Thank you, sir. I'm sure you're right."

"Of course I am. I know my own daughter. Sivorne's highly strung—she takes after her mother in that, of course—but she's strong beneath it all. She'll come through, never you fear. Now," he added conspiratorially, "why don't you go along and see her for a few minutes before she takes her rest? It'll be your last chance, you know: the women won't be joining us again, as it's bad luck for them to mingle with the men on a wedding eve."

Anyr nodded and his smile became more relaxed. "I'll take your advice, sir. Thank you again.

If you'll both excuse me . . ." He crossed the hall, his step lighter than it might have been a few minutes earlier, and when he had gone Aronin looked at Raerche and gave a long sigh.

"I'd thought of suggesting that we might postpone the wedding for a little while under the circumstances," he said. "However, if you really feel that Sivorne will be all right . . ."

"Of course she will," Raerche reassured him. "Besides, Maiv would never countenance such an idea." He raised his eyebrows slightly, indicating without the need for words how unwise it would be to cross Maiv. "And neither would Sivorne. I know her. Just like her mother." He smiled fondly. "*Just* like her mother."

Aronin chuckled, then turned to a small table that stood near the hearth. "Well, we can take our ease now until tomorrow. To that end, I've recently taken delivery of a particularly fine wine that I'd value your opinion of. Will you take a glass with me now?"

Raerche beamed and patted his midriff. "Yes, my friend, I do believe I will!"

Maiv personally prepared Sivorne's hot herbal drink that night. The servants were overawed by her presence in the kitchen, where their masters rarely if ever ventured, and kept a respectful distance as she busied herself with the brew. When it was ready Maiv turned and courteously thanked the cook—who was, after all, the uncrowned queen of this below-stairs realm—for the use of her domain. And as she did so, no one saw the plain little drudge of a serving-maid who darted forward and dropped an extra pinch of powdered herbs into the cup which Maiv had prepared.

Ghysla, in her servant's guise, had watched these small rituals very carefully. She had seen which herbs were added to Sivorne's drink each evening to make her sleep, and though she couldn't read the labels on the jars, she had memorized their locations on the kitchen shelves. It had been easy amid the general chaos to steal a small portion of each herb, and easy now to add what she had stolen to the cup as Maiv exchanged courtesies with the cook. With at least a double dose of the soporific powders in her drink, Sivorne would sleep very soundly indeed tonight. And that was exactly what Ghysla wanted.

The hour of waiting, between the moment when the last yawning steward went to bed and the moment when she judged it safe to emerge from hiding, seemed one of the longest hours in Ghysla's entire life. She crouched in the outhouse, shivering at the sly nip of the wind blowing through the rickety door, and watched the moon as it climbed slowly into the sky. At last she felt it safe to emerge, and crept through the silent kitchen and up the stairs into the body of the darkened house. Her heart was pounding with excitement as she made her way through the hall and up the main staircase, then along the maze of passages to Sivorne's turret. Pausing at the foot of the spiral flight, she suffered a terrible moment when her nerve almost failed her. She couldn't do this! a small inner voice protested. What if something were to go wrong? What if she were to fail in her deception and be found out? But then a second voice surged up within her, arguing fiercely. Was she a complete fool and coward, to falter now? The risk was worthwhile, for if she didn't go through with her plan, then she would lose Anyr surely and forever. There would be no second chance, not once he was wed to the real Sivorne, and to turn tail and run when she was so close to fulfilling her dream would be madness. She *must* do it. Otherwise, she would live out the rest of her miserable life with the agonizing knowledge that she had thrown away her one chance to achieve her own heart's desire and his. That would be beyond bearing.

Ghysla took a very deep breath and started up the stairs. At the top she stood for several minutes outside Sivorne's door with one ear pressed to the wood, listening for any sound from within. There was nothing, and at last she pushed down her terrors and lifted the latch. The door swung open, and she saw Sivorne, her face dimly lit by the one low lantern that her mother had left burning, fast asleep in the bed.

Now: the final test. Ghysla tiptoed across the room and bent over the bed. Then she breathed, very gently, on the sleeping girl's face. Sivorne didn't stir, and Ghysla's confidence grew. Reaching out, she touched Sivorne's cheek. Still no reaction, and still nothing when, further emboldened, she shook her gently by the shoulder. All was well; the sleeping draught had done its work thoroughly. All she had to do now was remove the drugged girl, and take her place.

She darted to the window, pulled back the curtain and cajoled the casement open. Cold air rushed in, and Ghysla leaned over the sill, looking down at the giddying drop below. She could see patterns of white foam in the dark as the sea beat against the rocks at the foot of the great cliff, and the hungry sound of it was like grim, deep voices singing in unearthly chorus. Ghysla ran back to the bed and with one movement wrenched the blankets from Sivorne's sleeping form. The girl was wearing a nightgown of fine white lawn decorated with lace. For a moment Ghysla couldn't resist pausing to finger the delicate fabric in wonder and envy, but then with an effort she snapped her mind back to more urgent matters and, grasping Sivorne under the arms, hauled her out of bed and across the floor. Grunting with effort, and with the awkwardness of lifting the girl's limp body, she heaved her part way over the sill then paused for breath. One more powerful push and Sivorne would tumble from the window like a frail white bird, turning over and over and falling down to the waiting sea. The currents would take her body and sweep it far away to the west, and no one would ever know what had become of her. So easy. Just one push . . .

With a cold little clutching at her heart, Ghysla relized that she couldn't do it. She couldn't kill this girl in cold blood—by all the old gods, she thought, she wouldn't even be able to do it in the heat of passion, for she had murdered Coorla that way and the thought of having another such deed on her conscience nearly froze her blood. Back in the mountains, when she'd first set eyes on Sivorne, she had fervently wished the girl dead; but there was a vast chasm of difference between a prayer to the elemental forces and having Sivorne's blood on her own hands. After all, she reasoned dismally, what harm had Sivorne done, other than fall in love with Anyr? If that was a crime, than she herself was every bit as guilty. She couldn't kill her. It was wrong, evil. She couldn't do it!

But if her nature rebelled against cold murder, what *was* she to do? Abandon her plan, and with it all her hopes and dreams? She'd already wrangled through that argument and knew that she couldn't bear to give up her chance of winning Anyr. Sivorne must at the very least be taken far away from this house and hidden in a place from which she couldn't escape and where no one would ever find her. There were a hundred such locations in this wild land—but the solution wouldn't work, for how could Ghysla cope with the necessities of keeping Sivorne alive? She couldn't steel her already ravaged conscience to the idea of leaving the girl to starve to death, yet neither could she bear the thought of keeping her a prisoner for the rest of her life.

For some minutes she stood by the window, gnawing at her long, clawlike nails in a silent turmoil of indecision. Sivorne was still slumped over the sill, the wind lifting her golden hair and blowing it about her head like a halo. *One push,* Ghysla thought again; then as quickly thrust the dreadful idea away, this time for good. There was another answer. There *had* to be.

Then it came to her. Something that would salve her conscience—yes, that again—but still allow her to go through with her scheme. Killing Sivorne was out of the question, yet keeping her a living prisoner seemed equally impossible. But there was a middle way, a way that lay between life and death, and to one who remembered the old magics from the time before the humans came, that way was still open. Sivorne wouldn't be harmed; indeed, she'd have no knowledge of her fate, for she would be in a sleep that could endure without hurt for centuries if need be. Ghysla smiled. She would take Sivorne away to her cave in the peaks by Kelda's Horns, and there she would lay the sleep upon her. The old sleep. The great sleep. The Sleep of Stone.

She approached the unconscious girl again and tried to lift her. Sivorne was slender and light by human standards, but none the less her weight was a great strain on Ghysla's thin arms. She wondered if she would have the strength to fly to the mountains with such a burden, but pushed the doubts firmly down. She was strong enough. And it was night, the time when she was at her best; her friends the elements would aid her and the silver light of the moon, night's undisputed queen, would lend her power.

Ghysla slipped her hands more firmly under Sivorne's arms and whispered, in her own tongue, "*Queen Moon, please aid me now!*" Then, clenching her teeth, she heaved with all her strength and lifted Sivorne with her as she scrambled up on to the window sill. Praying that she hadn't overestimated her ability, she poised for one second over the dizzying drop then launched herself into the air.

Her wings beat, faltered as Sivorne's dead weight wrenched her arms, then her grip tightened and her wings beat again more strongly. She was gaining height—she was soaring away from the house—yes, she thought exultantly, yes, I can do it, I can do it!

Like an unearthly bird of prey, with the limp girl in her arms, Ghysla flew away toward the west.

The cave was the closest thing that Ghysla had ever had to a home of her own. High up among the crags, it looked out over a stupendous vista of mountain slopes and green valleys, with the sea a glittering silver dagger beyond. The cave had no furnishings—she wouldn't have known what to do with such things, even if she could have come by them—but a natural shelf in one sheltered corner, piled high with heather to keep her warm, made a serviceable if rough bed which served her simple needs well enough.

She swooped to the ledge at the cave's mouth, and released her burden with a gasp of relief. The flight had taxed her enormously and for some minutes all she could do was crouch on all fours on the rock, her arms rigid with agony and her lungs heaving as she struggled to regain her breath. At last she rose, steeled herself for the final effort and, staggering under the weight, carried Sivorne into the cave itself. She laid the girl on the rough heather bed, arranged her hands in a folded position over her breast, then stepped back. She knew the spell even though she'd never used it before, and her huge, unhuman eyes glazed over as though suddenly the physical world had become invisible to her and she was staring into another, far stranger realm.

Softly at first, then with increasing strength and confidence, Ghysla began to chant. The words she spoke, and the language she used, were old beyond imagining, and as the syllables of her spell wound and wove through the cave it seemed that strange, half-seen forms took shape in the dimness, shadow-ghosts out of a long-forgotten age when ancient gods had ruled and ancient laws had held sway. On the bed of heather, the appearance of the golden-haired girl in her white lawn gown began slowly to alter. At first the changes were so subtle that an unpracticed eye wouldn't have noticed them, but then, as Ghysla chanted on, they became more and more unequivocal. The fine color of Sivorne's hair was fading to a paler, duller hue, like the sand of a sunless cove. The white lawn gown was turning to grey. Her skin was losing its delicate bloom and becoming first like parchment, then like marble. At last the few stray tresses of hair which the night breeze and Ghysla's breath had been stirring faintly at Sivorne's cheeks and brow froze in midmotion and were still—and Ghysla knew that her task was complete.

The words of the spell faded away into a last echo, and the cave was steeped in silence. Very slowly, Ghysla moved to stand beside the heather bed. And there, beautiful still, but cold and unaware and no longer human, Sivorne lay transformed into a statue of solid stone.

For a long time Ghysla gazed down at her. Sivorne was not dead, she knew; instead her living essence had entered a realm of profound and dreamless sleep, and there she might stay, undisturbed, yet never aging or dying, for ten or a hundred or a thousand years. It was done. Ghysla's conscience tried one last time to protest the injustice of her deed, but its voice was small and weak, and she pushed it aside and let it drown in the happiness of her triumph.

"Thank you," she whispered to the old gods and the old powers who had come to her aid tonight. *"Thank you!"*

Filled with a sudden surge of new energy and excitement, she ran from the cave and launched herself away into the sky, soaring back toward Caris.

CHAPTER VI

The morning of the wedding dawned fine and fair with a glorious sunrise. From daybreak the house of Caris was a hive of activity; breakfast was a hastily snatched affair for masters and servants alike, and by the time the sun showed its face above the inland moors the final preparations were almost complete. The great hall was filled with flowers, and a long carpet had been laid to form a central aisle along which the bridal procession would walk. Wine, ale, and sweetmeats had been made ready in two anterooms for early coming guests, and in another small room two fiddlers, a piper, and a bass viol player tuned their instruments and prepared their music.

Anyr was in his own bedchamber, attended by two manservants who had laid out his wedding clothes and were now attending to his bath. He was as nervous as a pent thoroughbred horse as again and again he ran through in his mind what he must do, what he must say—but his trepidation was nothing compared to the terrors of the girl who stood in the high turret room in another part of the house, surrounded by a bevy of excited, chattering women.

Ghysla felt as though she were dreaming. Early this morning, when a curtseying maid had brought her a breakfast of honey cakes and herb tea and had greeted with her a deferential "good day, madam," the full enormity of what she had achieved had come home to her for the first time. To the maid, she was without question Sivorne. And today she was to wed her beloved Anyr.

She hadn't touched the drink or the cakes. To her relief the maidservant had quickly left her alone, and she used the time—which would, she knew, be short enough—to gather her wits, calm her racing pulse as far as she could, and ensure that the role she must play and the image she must maintain were as firmly fixed in her consciousness as it was possible for them to be. Then came a knocking on her door. Guessing the identity of her visitor, Ghysla took a deep breath, whispered a fervent prayer to the old gods, and raised her head to face her first ordeal.

The door opened and Maiv entered the room. For a split second Ghysla's courage almost failed her, but she redoubled her grip on herself and—help me now, oh, help me now!—smiled Sivorne's sweetest smile.

"My dear child!" Maiv crossed the room and kissed her cheek, a strange and almost shocking sensation to Ghysla, who had never in her life been kissed before, let alone by a human. Then

Maiv stood back, studying her anxiously. "How are you today?"

This was the greatest test. Ghysla swallowed something that was trying to stick in her throat, and said in Sivorne's light, young voice, "I am very well, Mother!"

Maiv hesitated, and a hint of doubt crept into her eyes. "You're quite sure, now? No nightmares? No fears?"

Ghysla shook her head, feeling the golden hair ripple on her shoulders. "No, Mother, none. I feel . . . I feel vastly recovered."

"Well, that's splendid news!" Maiv visibly relaxed—but the doubt in her eyes lingered just long enough to strike a thin icicle of fright into Ghysla's heart. Quickly she turned her head away, terrified that she had overlooked some small but vital detail which Sivorne's mother alone would recognize, and she heard Maiv's footsteps crossing the room.

"You haven't touched your breakfast."

Ghysla risked looking up again and saw the woman gazing at the covered tray. "I'm not hungry, Mother. I truly couldn't eat a thing."

"Well, with all the excitement I suppose it's not surprising; though you should try to have something or you may feel faint later. Still, I'm sure that can be put right after the ceremony." Maiv smiled at her. "The women will be coming shortly to attend you, and they'll bring hot water and scented herbs for your bath. I must go and attend to my own preparations." Another pause.

"You're quite *sure* there's nothing amiss? If you'd prefer me to stay . . ."

Gods, no! Ghysla thought in horror. Aloud, she said, "No, Mother, I'm well and fine, really I am."

"Then I'll leave you in the servants' capable hands." Maiv gave her a second long, thoughtful stare, and Ghysla hid her hands under the bedclothes as they suddenly began to tremble. Then Maiv looked away.

"I'll come back and see you when you're dressed and ready. Send the tirewoman to my room if you want me in the meantime, and I'll make sure your father is waiting to escort you downstairs at the right hour. And don't be nervous, my dear child. This will be a joyful day for us all!"

As she descended the turret stairs, Maiv met the tirewoman coming up, accompanied by three maids with jugs of steaming water. The tirewoman curtsied. "How is Mistress Sivorne this morning, madam?"

"She's greatly better, I'm thankful to say. At least . . ." Maive frowned and the woman prompted, "Madam?"

"Oh, I'm sure it's nothing; simply the nervousness we might expect of her on such a day. But . . ." There was something else nagging at the back of Maiv's mind, something she couldn't quite pinpoint. What could it be? Oh, this was foolish; after the alarms of the last few days she was letting her imagination run away with her and seeing ghosts in the shadows. With an effort she forced her expression to clear, and smiled reassuringly at the tirewoman. "I'm sure there's nothing to worry about. Sivorne just isn't *quite* herself yet."

She swept on down the stairs as the women went on their way.

She was ready. Trembling with sick nerves, keyed up with mingled terror and excitement to the point where she thought she must surely shatter into a thousand pieces; but ready. And not once had her disguise slipped, not once had the women who flapped about her like hens in a coop suspected that anything was remotely amiss. The gown, a wonderful creation of silk and lace and tiny pearls, had been fastened about her, silk shoes had been slipped on to her feet, and her golden hair had been brushed and combed and braided and looped before finally the silver chaplet adorned with flowers was set upon her head like a crown and the lace veil draped over it to cover her face and frame her in mystery as though she were a goddess. Radiant, her cheeks flushed, she smiled dazzlingly as the women exclaimed over her. Then, through the window which they had opened to let in the fresh morning air, she heard a sound that set her heart racing and rushing within her. The sound of a joyful, clamorous carillon, as all the bells in the harbor town began to ring out in celebration of her marriage day.

The door of the bedchamber opened, and Raerche and Maiv stood upon the threshold.

"Sivorne!" Raerche came forward to embrace her, and was clucked at by the women who were anxious that the wonderful bridal gown shouldn't be crumpled. In the background Maiv, resplendent in crimson and with jewels in her hair, smiled proudly and dabbed at her eyes.

"They are waiting, child," Raerche told her. "Are you ready?"

Ghysla nodded, barely able to speak for the dryness of her throat. "Yes," she whispered. "Yes ... Father."

She laid her arm over his as she had seen the real Sivorne do at the rehearsal, and slowly, solemnly, they set off down the spiral steps and along the passage to the main staircase. They reached the top of the flight, and Ghysla saw that there were people waiting below; Aronin, six young girls dressed in green, a group of musicians, and a tall, thin stooped man in a brown robe which she recognized as the garb of a priest of the humans' new gods. Involuntarily her hand tightened on Raerche's arm, and he patted her fingers reassuringly. Then they were descending, her legs threatening to give way under her with every step, and as they reached the flagstoned floor the musicians raised their instruments and struck up a slow, stately tune. The bridal procession formed up; the priest at its head, Aronin following, then Ghysla, flanked by Raerche and Maiv, and lastly the six young girls like a flowing wave in their wake. Then the doors of the great hall were thrown open from within, spilling out a blaze of torchlight. Ghysla had a momentary, dazzling impression of a great throng of people turning to stare at her, their fine clothes a sea of brilliant color, and of a seemingly endless blue-carpeted aisle stretching straight as a moonshaft ahead. And at the far end of the hall she saw a lone figure, quietly magnificent in green and gold, and though the distance between them was too great for his face to be so clear, she was certain that his gaze fastened upon her, and that he smiled a warm and joyous smile that was meant for her alone.

Suddenly all Ghysla's fear evaporated, and her courage and confidence came surging back. This was the moment she had plotted for, striven for—even, she thought, steeling herself, killed for. Her long-cherished dream was coming true. In just a few short minutes from now, Anyr would be her very own, forever.

So softly that no one could hear her, she whispered his name. And with her white arm upon the arm of Raerche, and her vivid blue eyes shining with happiness beneath the lace veil, she walked down the carpeted aisle between the ranks of guests, to join her beloved.

Anyr stepped forward as the party reached the end of the hall, and his hands reached out to Ghysla. She took his fingers, and together they turned and stepped on to a square of cloth, embroidered with sacred sigils, which the priest had brought from his temple. The music ended as the priest himself took his place before them, and a hush fell in the hall. Then the priest raised his hands heavenward.

"I call upon the gods to witness that this is a day of joy and celebration!" he declared. "And I call upon the powers of the heavens above us, and the powers of the earth beneath us, and the powers of the sea around us, to bring good fortune and all blessing upon this son of man and this daughter of woman who have come within the gods' sight to vow and pledge their troth to one another."

As he spoke the opening words of the ritual Ghysla felt a sharp stab of fear. *Human magic—* it was inimical to her, it had terrible power to harm her! If this man called on the humans' gods—

But then she remembered that he was a priest, not a sorcerer. She knew about priests; they had no power and no magic, they were simply speakers of fine words, mere servants and not avatars of the new gods. She was safe.

The priest completed his blessing, then intoned a short homily on the solemn responsibilities that a wife and husband must share. Anyr fidgeted nervously and, greatly daring now that she knew she had nothing to fear from the holy man, Ghysla squeezed his hand reassuringly. He flicked her a quick, grateful smile that warmed her like the sun's rays, then squared his shoulders and faced forward again as the next and most important part of the ceremony began.

"Anyr of the House of Caris. Whom do you name as your sponsor and your witness on this happy day?"

Anyr cleared his throat. "I name the Lord Aronin of Caris as my sponsor, whom I am privileged to call my sire."

Aronin stepped forward, beaming, and the priest said, "Aronin, Lord of Caris, do you freely and gladly consent to the joining of your son in wedlock to Sivorne?"

"I freely and gladly consent to it!"

Ghysla's pulse quickened to a rapid, painful beat as the priest's gaze turned now to her. "Sivorne of the Eastern Inlands. Whom do you name as your sponsor and your witness on this happy day?"

For an awful moment Ghysla thought she wouldn't be able to speak. Her throat was dry and her body was trembling. But the words she had heard at the rehearsal came back clearly to her, and with a rush of relief she felt the constriction ease and heard Sivorne's well-modulated voice speak from her own lips.

"I name Maiv, wife of Raerche, as my sponsor, whom I am privileged to call my mother."

Maiv moved to stand at her side, her figure a blur of crimson through the veil, and the priest asked, "Maiv, wife of Raerche, do you freely and gladly consent to the joining of your daughter in wedlock to Anyr?"

There was a pause. Then Maiv answered: "I freely and gladly consent to it." She stepped forward, turned to face Ghysla and lifted the veil away from her face. Ghysla blinked with Sivorne's blue eyes, and Maiv's own eyes narrowed slightly as though in puzzlement. Then with a small shake of her head, as though she were casting off some unwonted thought or trouble, she moved back to her place.

The priest held out his hands. "I now ask Anyr and Sivorne to face each other, and to join their hands for the speaking of the holy pledge."

For the first time, without the veil to impede her, Ghysla looked up into Anyr's face. He smiled reassuringly . . . then the smile seemed to falter for a moment before he regained his self-control. He was even more nervous than she herself, Ghysla realized with a surge of deep affection. Poor, beloved Anyr. When this ritual was over she would be so kind to him, she would soothe him, stroke his brow, serve him, love him, make him so happy. He'd never again need to be afraid of anything.

"Sivorne of the Eastern Inland." The priest was speaking again, and he laid a hand gently on the crown of Ghysla's head, making the flowers of her chaplet rustle with a pleasant sound. "I ask you to repeat these words after me. I, Sivorne, daughter of Raerche and daughter of Maiv . . ."

Feeling that her heart might burst with happiness, Ghysla began to repeat aloud the words she had so longed to say; the words which would bind her to Anyr. "I, Sivorne, daughter of Raerche and daughter of Maiv . . . Do forswear all other love and all other duty for my love for and duty to Anyr of Caris . . . I shall be wife and helpmeet, comforter and nurturer . . . I shall do him all honor as my husband and my lord . . . He shall be the sun of my days, the moon of my nights . . . And I pledge and promise that in my eyes there shall be no other beloved, from this day until the day of my last rest."

She was shaking, shivering, the thrill of the words and what they meant coursing ecstatically through her. The priest, aware of her excitement, smiled with faint amusement but kept his voice appropriately solemn as he turned to Anyr.

"Anyr of the House of Caris. Sivorne of the Eastern Inland has pledged her troth to you, and so now in your turn I ask you to repeat these words after me. I, Anyr, son of Aronin and son of the departed Elona . . ."

The tip of Anyr's tongue touched his lower lip. The congregation waited.

"I, Anyr . . ." Another, longer hesitation. "Son of Aronin and son of the departed Elona . . ."

"Do forswear all other love and all other duty for my love for and duty to Sivorne of the Eastern Inland."

"Do forswear . . ." Anyr's hands, which still held Sivorne's, suddenly began to shake; then with no warning he snatched his fingers out of her grip. The color had drained from his face, leaving it pasty and unhealthy-looking, and his eyes were wild, like the eyes of a cornered animal.

The priest, disconcerted, leaned forward. "My son, there's no need to be nervous. Repeat the words now, after me: 'do forswear all other love and all other duty'—"

"No!" Anyr's voice cut shockingly through the hall like a honed knife and he took two stumbling paces backward, away from the priest, away from Ghysla. "No! I won't say them!"

"Anyr!" Aronin, his face a study in shock, hastened to his son's side and gripped his arm. "Anyr, what is it, what's wrong?"

Anyr threw his father's restraining hand off and pointed at Ghysla, who shrank back in horror from his state.

"You!" he said in a harsh, emotional voice. "I don't know who you are, or what you are. *But you are not my true bride!*"

CHAPTER VII

There was an appalled silence. Then, like an explosion, the hiatus was shattered by a roar of fury.

"What is this?" Raerche thrust his way past Maiv and past the dismayed priest to confront Anyr. "What is this, boy? What are you saying? How *dare* you offer such an insult to my daughter?"

Anyr stared back at him, unflinching, but before he could reply Aronin stepped forward. "Now wait, Raerche! I don't know what this is all about any more than you, but—"

Raerche turned on him, white-lipped. "You heard what the whelp said! He slights my daughter, and he slights my family!"

"You have the temerity to call my son a whelp—" Aronin countered, his face purpling with indignation.

"I call him whelp and more! He—"

"Wait!" The single, emphatic word cut through the rising tide of anger, and the two older men stopped in midflow as they both recognized

Maiv's voice. They drew back in chagrin as she stepped between them and Anyr and, her face pale, Maiv turned to look at Anyr. There was both sympathy and fear in her expression.

"Anyr," she said in a quiet tone which nonetheless silenced the whisperings that had begun to fill the hall. "Explain to me what you meant."

Anyr looked ill. "I . . ." Then he faltered. Maiv flicked a swift glance at Ghysla, who throughout the exchange had stood frozen by blind horror, then her gaze returned to Anyr's face. "Perhaps," she continued gently, seeing that Anyr still couldn't bring himself to speak, "I can answer the question for you. Are you saying that this girl is *not* Sivorne?"

Aronin swore a soft, shocked oath. Anyr hissed through clenched teeth, then abruptly nodded. "Yes, lady," he said unhappily. "That is what I meant."

Raerche exploded, "Good gods, the boy's gone mad!" but Maiv turned sharply on him.

"No, husband; I don't believe he has. Or if he has, then so have I—because I believe him."

"*What*? Damn my eyes, this is—"

Again Maiv interrupted him. "*Listen* to me, Raerche! I knew something was wrong; I've known it since I first went to Sivorne's bedchamber this morning, but I couldn't find the root of it and so I tried to dismiss it from my mind. But I couldn't. I know my own daughter better than any other living soul knows her, and I know—I *feel*—that this is not the same girl I kissed good-night last evening!"

Raerche started to protest again, and even Aronin, from defending Anyr, was starting to express doubts at what seemed, by the standards of all reason, a wildly impossible claim. Amid their arguments, however, Maiv turned her back on them and looked at Ghysla.

"Ask her a question," she said. "Ask her a question to which only Sivorne could know the answer."

Raerche's tirade collapsed and he stood with his jaw working soundlessly.

"Ask her," Maiv said again. "If she answers you rightly, you may lock me away for a mad-woman. But ask her. Or if you won't, I will." Her eyes narrowed with pain and anger, but also with determination, and she addressed Ghysla directly for the first time.

"Sivorne—or whoever you are. When you were twelve years old, your little sister died of a fever. What was her name?"

Ghysla stared back at her. She couldn't move; she hadn't been able to move, to speak, to react in any way whatsoever since the hideous moment when Anyr had refused to make his vow and had turned on her. She'd lived in terror that her deception would be discovered, but she'd never once dreamed that Anyr would be the one to unmask her. He hadn't realized who she was, he hadn't understood what was happening; now, unwittingly, he had ruined everything! She felt as though she were drowning under a tidal wave, but however hard she fought and struggled she couldn't break the stranglehold of grief and misery and terror that held her utterly helpless. Before her, five faces—Maiv, Raerche, Aronin, the priest, and worst, by far the worst of all, Anyr— stared at her like demons staring out of some monstrous otherworld. Behind her and to either side was a sea of craning people, the wedding guests who minutes ago had adored her but who now seemed to her fevered mind to be turning into a predatory pack closing in on her. There was no escape route. She couldn't turn and run or fly. She was surrounded, trapped, cornered. Her dream had suddenly and violently become a nightmare.

Her tongue, unbidden, started to quiver in her mouth and an ugly sound broke from her throat. "Nnn. . . . nnn . . ."

Maiv stared at her, implacable. "What was that? What did you say?"

Staring; the woman was staring at her, like a judge condemning her for a crime . . . "Nnnn . . . nn-aaaa—" She couldn't control herself, the noises were vomiting up from the depths of her soul and she couldn't stem them. Tears welled in her eyes and began to stream down her cheeks—and suddenly her eyes weren't blue and lovely, but huge and owllike and alien. And her skin was no longer pale and smooth, and her hair was no longer golden, and her teeth were sharp, and from her bony shoulders wings were growing—

"*Nnnn* . . . *aahh!*" Ghysla's voice—her *own* voice—rose to a howl of despair and misery. "*Nnnn* . . . *aaAAAAHH!*"

Aronin yelled in horror, "*Gods defend us!*" and women started to scream as, in all Sivorne's wedding finery, Ghysla finally and hideously metamorphosed back into her own form. Maiv, who stood a bare pace in front of her and so bore the full impact of the terrible sight, gave a thin shriek, rolled up her eyes and dropped to the floor in a dead faint. The priest, making frantic signs against evil, backed away like a frightened rabbit. And Anyr—Anyr was staring transfixed at Ghysla, and in his eyes was stunned, inexpressible horror.

Then, cutting through the uproar, Aronin's stentorian voice bellowed out. "Kill that thing! *Kill it!*"

Steel rattled as the men nearest to him drew their swords, and three blades flashed toward Ghysla. Her paralysis snapped and she skittered backward, flinging her hands up to protect herself and screeching a protest. The swordsmen started after her, but suddenly Anyr cried, "No, wait!"

The men hesitated, and Anyr pushed past them them to where Ghysla had tripped over the hem of Sivorne's wedding gown, stumbled and fallen ungracefully to the floor. He stood over her, his face twisted with loathing, and demanded in a shaking voice, "*Where is my Sivorne? What have you done with her?*"

Ghysla whimpered. Her Anyr, her beloved, was speaking to her, but not with the warmth and kindness she had dreamed of hearing from his lips. This wasn't love: It was hatred. And her heart couldn't bear it.

"Please . . . she whispered, and began to crawl clumsily towards him. "*Please*—Anyr, my love, my dear one, don't you know me?"

"*Know* you?" Anyr recoiled, shuddering. "No! I've never seen such a thing as you before in all my life! What are you—in all the gods' names, *what are you?*"

"I am your true beloved! I am Ghysla, Anyr, I am *Ghysla!*" Then she saw that that meant nothing to him. "Oh, but you don't know my name, do you? You still don't *realize* . . ."

And suddenly, shockingly, where Ghysla's grotesque figure had been standing, a brindle seal appeared. It's great eyes gazed mournfully into Anyr's, and then it became a fallow deer, then a hare, then a bird, then a vixen—

"Stop it!" Anyr covered his face with both hands. "*Stop it!*"

Dismayed, Ghysla reverted back to her own shape. "You must know me now, Anyr!" she cried desperately. "I am your seal, your young doe, your songbird; I am all the creatures you befriended! And you love me—I know you love me, for you have told me so a hundred times and more! I am Ghysla, your true and only love, and now I've come to you to be your bride!"

Slowly, understanding began to dawn in Anyr's eyes, and with it stark horror. "Oh, no . . ." he whispered. "No, *no*—dear gods, this is a nightmare, it can't be *true!*"

Still not comprehending the truth, Ghysla reached out toward him. "It isn't a nightmare, dearest Anyr, it's real! I love you just as you love me! I love you with all my heart and all my soul, and now you won't have to marry Sivorne, because she's gone!" Anyr opened his mouth, but before he could speak she drew a racking breath and rushed on. "I took her away, I took her far away to a place where she'll never trouble you again! Now *I* can be your wife instead. I don't need to look like this—I can be as beautiful as you want me to be; I have power, I know the magics, I can be anything and everything for you!" Her hands, stretching out imploringly, caught at the hem of his cloak. "We'll be so happy, Anyr, we'll be together now for always, don't you see?"

Anyr continued to stare at her—then suddenly he reached out and took hold of her arms. For one glorious moment Ghysla thought that at last he had understood, that he would pull her to him and embrace her, as he did in her dreams every night, and that everything would be all right. But then he spoke, and the words he uttered, in a terrible, choking voice, shattered the dream into a thousand shards.

He said: "Where is my Sivorne? *What have you done with her?*"

The ferocious question stabbed Ghysla as surely and as agonizingly as any sword could have done, and her eyes widened uncomprehendingly. "But you don't care about her, Anyr! You love *me!*"

"You?" Anyr made an awful gagging sound. "Gods blind me, what kind of madness is this? How could I ever love you? You're not even human!" He released her as though her skin had suddenly become red hot, and his voice shook with a fury of emotion. "I love Sivorne, do you hear me? I love my sweet Sivorne! *And I want her back!*"

Ghysla began to tremble as the ugly truth finally broke down the barriers she had created and struck home. He was spurning her. Her beloved Anyr, her adored one, did not love her at all; instead he hated her, with a passion that matched the passion of her love for him. She couldn't believe it. She didn't *want* to believe it, she wouldn't, she *wouldn't*—and without warning a new emotion began to rise within her, overtaking her grief and swamping it. *Rage.* The rage of rejected love, the fury of faith and loyalty betrayed. She couldn't contain it and suddenly she didn't want to; all she wanted was to strike back at these humans who had treated her so cruelly; even at Anyr himself who had thrown her love for him back in her face like a piece of unwanted flotsam. And in the abject misery of his rejection, she had no more hope of controlling her reactions than she had of turning the sea tides in their endless course.

"No!" she yelled, with such violent intensity that Anyr rocked back on his heels. "No! No, NO, NO!"

There were cries of consternation as an electric charge of sparks crackled suddenly like a nimbus around her hair, and Ghysla leaped to her feet. "NO!" she screamed. "I'LL NEVER TELL YOU WHERE SHE IS! I'LL NEVER TELL YOU ANYTHING!" And she felt the magic, the old magic, rushing up in her like a torrent. People cried out in shock as the sacred embroidered cloth on which she and Anyr had stood such a short time ago shot into the air as though a tornado had snatched it from the floor. Wind buffeted through the hall, sending several of the guests reeling; the cloth twisted itself into a tortured knot and then ripped in half, the two fragments flying away in opposite directions. Ghysla grinned horribly, showing her pointed teeth, and on the far side of the hall a chair leaped from its place, somersaulted and struck an elderly man on the head. The curtains began to billow like sails in a storm, trying to tear themselves from their moorings; then, as one, three of the flower vases that decked the hall toppled over and smashed, while the flowers themselves flew upward to perform a mad dance in midair. A table started to rise slowly, menacingly from the floor, and there was pandemonium as those beneath it fell over each other in their efforts to get out of the way. Ghysla's terrible smile widened until it seemed her face must crack in two: then the double doors burst open with a shattering crash and a bizarre assortment of objects, from mats and furniture to plates of food, jugs of wine, and even flagstones from the floor, hurtled into the hall and flung themselves at the panicking guests. They struck with deadly accuracy, felling several unfortunates before the others collected their wits sufficiently to fend off the attacks, and Ghysla shrieked with hysterical laughter as she saw the mayhem she was causing.

"More!" she howled. *"More!"* The hinges of the doors themselves groaned as she flung a powerbolt at them; acrid smoke rose in a choking cloud as the metal began to melt. Then from the corner of her eye she saw two men, bolder and sharper-witted than the rest, running at her with swords drawn. She let out a fearsome screech and turned on them; her eyes blazed black and then yellow, and a second bolt of power blasted between her two attackers and threw them both thirty feet across the floor. Ghysla spun about, looking for new assailants and daring anyone to risk the same fate—and realized that no one was going to meet her challenge. Instead, the wedding guests were stampeding toward the doors. She glimpsed the priest, his brown robe flapping, in the midst of the first terrified rush, and behind him were Raerche and two other men, support-

ing the barely conscious Maiv between them.
Ghysla started to laugh. She laughed, like the
demon Anyr had accused her of being, as the
dignified assembly collapsed into squealing,
scrambling chaos and the great hall emptied, and
she flung more bolts, and more, and more, yelling with a semblance of delight that only barely
kept the desolation in her soul at bay.

The last press of people burst through the
doors and ran for the sanctuary of the gardens.
Lord Aronin was among them, but on the threshold he stopped and looked back as he realized
that he had done all he could for his guests'
safety. Anyr saw him halt and ran back to his
side, calling two of the burliest servants to join
them, and all four stared at the scene in the hall.

The elegant room was in ruins. Tables and
chairs lay upturned and scattered, and the floor
was covered with a debris of smashed crockery,
dented pewter vessels, torn flowers and trampled
food. In the midst of the wreckage Ghysla stood
like a vision out of some demented nightmare.
The wedding veil was ripped and the chaplet of
flowers crushed among her hair's wild tangles;
and her skull-like face, vast eyes, and dark, membranous wings made a horrible contrast with the
lovely gown she wore. She looked alien and grotesque, a living paradox, an obscenity to human
sight.

Then she saw them, and her mouth opened in
a snarl, showing her savage teeth. Spittle drib-
bled over her lower lip—and, so swiftly that the

four men jumped with shock, she flung up her hands and a chair leaped from the floor and hurtled through the air straight at their heads. They ducked; the chair smashed against the doorframe, and Ghysla shrieked with frustration. Another violent gesture, and one of the heavy velvet curtains tore itself free from its hangings and shot across the room. But in her fury Ghysla had misjudged the spell, and as it billowed toward the four men the curtain brushed one of the glass-chimneyed lanterns that hung about the walls. The lantern fell, smashed; flame flared up as the oil spilled—and the curtain caught fire.

"Sweet gods!" Aronin cried hoarsely as he saw the danger. "The house—"

His words were drowned by a scream of terror from Ghysla. *She hadn't meant to do that!* She'd taken care to leave the lamps unscathed, but suddenly in her rage she'd lost control and now fire, her greatest enemy and her greatest dread, was blazing up in the hall and cutting her off from the main door.

The flames crackled, spreading rapidly and sending sparks fountaining upward. Smoke roiled, and Ghysla stumbled backward, her wings flapping and her hands beating frantically but ineffectually at the air before her in an attempt to ward off the horror. By the door Anyr was yelling for servants to bring brooms and water, but Aronin had seen Ghysla's reaction and he turned, shouting urgently to his son.

"Anyr! Anyr, look—the creature's afraid of

fire!" And before the astonished Anyr could stop him, he tore off his own cloak and ran into the hall, swinging the garment at the flames. It caught light and Lord Aronin dodged round the spreading blaze, brandishing the now burning cloak like a weapon. Ghysla saw him, shrieked again and darted for the smaller door at the far end of the hall. Servants were by now running to the scene; one quick-witted man saw what his master was doing and, while the others set to beating the flames out, made a makeshift torch of his own fire-broom and went to the lord's aid

Suddenly from the main doorway Anyr's voice rose above the mayhem. "Father, no! Father!" Steam hissed through the hall as a bucket of water was thrown on the blazing curtain; dodging the feet and brooms that trampled the flames, Anyr ran into the hall towards Aronin. "Father, wait! Stop!" Instinct was goading him and he didn't stop to rationalize; all he knew was that Ghysla should not be harmed.

But his plea came too late, for Ghysla had already fled through the door, and five men with Aronin at their head were pounding after her. The door slammed behind them before Anyr could reach it, and he stopped, breathless, chest heaving. They mustn't hurt her, he thought wildly. She alone knew what had become of Sivorne—and besides, an inner voice was telling him that, whatever she was and whatever she had done, to try to kill her would be a terrible injustice. He must go after them, he must stop them; and, pausing only a moment to catch his breath, he wrenched the door open once more and ran in his father's wake.

Ghysla raced desperately through the house, pursued by the five men who all carried the deadly, hated fire. She tried to escape down the passage that led to the kitchens, but one of the servants was too quick for her and blocked the way. Ghysla screeched, spun about and bolted toward a flight of stairs that rose to the upper floor. She didn't know where they would lead her and she didn't care; all that mattered was to get away from the flames. Behind her she heard Aronin's shout of triumph, then they were after her again and, stumbling, panicking, too frightened to reason, she raced for any sanctuary she could find.

She reached the top of the stairs and pelted along a deserted corridor. The men were gaining on her, shouting at her; she reached the end of the passage and swerved left, then saw a narrow archway and beyond it more steps, a spiral flight curving upward. The turrets—she remembered Sivorne's bedchamber and its high windows; she could escape that way, jump from the window and fly to safety!

Ghysla dived into the gap and, panting for breath, scrabbled her way up the staircase. She heard the men's voices behind her and she heard them laughing, but she didn't pause to wonder why. At last there was a door ahead of her; she fell on the latch, clawing at it; the door swung

open, and as the first of her pursuers appeared
around the curve in the stairs she flung herself
through the door and slammed it.

Light flared under the door in the narrow gap
between stone and wood. Forcing down the sick-
ness in her stomach, telling herself that she could
not, could *not* feel the heat of the flames beyond
the thin barrier, Ghysla found the bar, wrestled
it into place and backed slowly away across the
room, anticipating the first thunderous hammer-
ing of fists. But it didn't come. She knew the
men were there; she could hear their breathing,
hear the shuffling of feet, and shadows were
crossing the patch of light that spilled under the
door into the darkness.

Darkness ... suddenly she was gripped by a
terrible apprehension and, as though in mocking
confirmation, at the same moment she heard the
sound of a key being implacably turned in the
lock.

Slowly, very slowly, Ghysla turned around. And
a sound bubbled up in her throat, a low, dismal
moan that rose at last to a desolate and helpless
howl of utter misery.

Anyr heard the dreadful cry from the turret
room as he ran up the spiral stairs and the sound
made him shudder. His father was standing by
the turret-room door; he had dropped the re-
mains of his burning cloak and trodden out the
flames, and now he hung the bunch of keys back
on his belt. For a few moments he stared at the
door, until he had assured himself that Ghysla

would not use some magic and come bursting through to attack them. Then, his face grim, he turned to face Anyr.

"She won't escape from there," he said in a hard, flat voice.

Anyr swallowed. "She—isn't hurt?"

His father looked surprised, but shook his head. "No. She's as fit as any of us, more's the pity. We'll fix torches to the wall brackets here and leave them burning. Two of the men can stand guard until they're brought, to be on the safe side." Then his expression changed, and there was compassion in his eyes. "Come, my dear son. We must seek out Raerche and Maiv, and decide what's to be done."

Anyr nodded. His jaw was clenched and his eyes overly bright. If Aronin saw tears glittering there he said nothing of it, but only laid a sympathetic hand on the young man's shoulder as, with the other servants following at a tactful distance, they started back down the stairs. They left behind them two stone-faced sentries with their makeshift but effective torches. And on the other side of the locked door they left Ghysla, trapped and helpless as she knelt sobbing her despair in the lightless, windowless turret room.

CHAPTER VIII

Night fell on a grim scene outside the house of Caris. The gracious old building itself was in darkness, but all around it, in a circle broken only by the barrier of the cliffs, bonfires had been lit and their beacon glow illuminated the tense faces of an uneasy crowd.

Aronin had not allowed anyone to return to the house. It might be that there was no danger, he said, but he wasn't prepared to put any lives at risk until they knew more about the creature they had trapped in the turret room. The family and their guests and servants would find refuge with the townsfolk; in the meantime his first concern was to find a means of dealing with Ghysla.

The witches who only a few days ago had attended Sivorne had returned to the house, their numbers swelled now to a full traditional coterie of twenty-one. They had taken on the responsibility of feeding and tending the bonfires, and as they worked they chanted stern incantations against devils and gremlins of every kind. There was no doubt that their spells were having an effect, for soon after they began to chant, Ghysla had begun to howl horribly and shrilly from her high prison, her voice audible even through the turret's thick stone walls. But the witches' efforts had produced no more than that, and Aronin, at least, was convinced that they had reached a stalemate.

Maiv had recovered from her faint but was in shock, and had been taken to a local merchant's house where the physician was attending her. Raerche, after seeing her settled, had returned to Caris, and as the moon rose and the chanting continued he and Aronin drew aside from the anxious throng for a private discussion.

Anyr had not joined them. Earlier, Aronin had found him standing beside one of the bonfires, his stance rigid and his face a blank and stony mask as he stared fixedly at the turret where Ghysla was trapped. He wouldn't speak; but when Aronin looked into his eyes he saw clearly the anguish in his son's heart and knew that nothing save Sivorne's safe return could console him. And there, Aronin thought dismally, was the rub. They knew nothing of Sivorne's fate; all they could be sure of was that, whatever had become of her, the monstrosity in the tower was responsible—and the chances of persuading or forcing Ghysla to give up her secret were slender to say the very least. Thus far, no one had been able to bring themselves to speculate aloud on whether Sivorne might be alive or dead, Aronin had his own views and they weren't optimistic, but nothing would induce him to voice them either to Anyr or to Raerche. That, he felt, could only do more harm than good at a time like this. Better to concentrate on the demon, or whatever she was, and face the other, darker speculations later.

So he and Raerche wrangled with the problem of Ghysla while all around them the fires continued to burn and the witches continued to chant. The priest, fortified by several acolytes, was praying hard for the gods' intervention, but at a safe distance: he, Aronin thought with an edge of contempt, wouldn't have any practical solutions to offer. Nor did it seem likely that the witches would make much further progress. What, he asked himself desperately, was left?

A sudden murmuring among the onlookers nearby alerted him, and he and Raerche both looked up to see Anyr approaching through the crowd. People moved aside for him—one look at his face deterred them from trying to speak to him—and he strode to where the two older men stood.

"Father. Sir." He nodded briskly to them both, and Aronin saw that the misery in his eyes had been overtaken by a new emotion that combined anger and a bleak but unshakeable determination. "This won't work."

Aronin sighed. "I know, lad, I know. The women are doing their best, but—"

"But their best isn't enough. We must take

stronger measures." Anyr paused. "There's only one thing left to us. We must call in a sorcerer."

Shocked, Raerche made a religious sign, and Aronin looked at his son in chagrin. "Anyr, that's out of the question! You know our priests' teachings as well as I do! Our forefathers have shunned the practice of sorcery for generations past, and now you say we should resort to it again? It's dark magic, and I won't hear of it!"

"But how else are we going to break this deadlock?" Anyr argued. "It's our only hope of finding Sivorne. We *must* do it!"

"It's too dangerous! Besides, where would you find a sorcerer in this day and age? They're all long dead!"

"Not all, Father. There's still Mornan."

Aronin's jaw dropped. "Mornan the recluse? But he's—he's—"

"He's a sorcerer, and by all accounts a powerful one. I know he doesn't practice, at least not openly; that's why we've left him alone all these years. But if he can be persuaded to help us—"

Aronin snorted. "Persuade Mornan to help anyone? You might as well ask the sun not to rise tomorrow!"

"But isn't it worth *trying*? Sivorne may still be alive! Father, listen to me—we must do this, for her sake!" Anyr turned in desperate appeal to Raerche. "Sir, you agree with me, don't you? I don't care about the danger, I don't care what manner of risk we might be taking—if sorcery can help Sivorne, then we must use sorcery! We have to try anything, *anything* that might save her!"

Aronin saw an answering emotion kindle in Raerche's expression, and he gave way. "I don't like the idea," he said unhappily. "I don't like it, and I don't trust it. But ... oh, gods, perhaps you're right, my son. Perhaps it's our only hope. Though what it might take to move the heart of a man like Mornan I don't know."

"I'll make him help us," Anyr threw a quick glance over his shoulder toward the tower, where Ghysla's cries were still audible above the chanting. "Whether it takes bribery or the point of a sword, I'll do it somehow."

And before either of the two older men could say another word, he was running toward the stable block and yelling for his horse.

Mornan—no one knew if he had any other name—lived in a secluded old manse four miles outside Caris. For years now he hadn't once left his domain, and only the fact that the provender, calling once a month, still found a small pile of silver and a curt note ordering modest food supplies outside the manse gates, proved that he was still alive. How he lived and what he did with his time was a mystery; he employed no servants and received no visitors, and there were no rumors of sorcerous workings in or around the solitary old house. The townsfolk largely ignored him; only a few of the eldest inhabitants, prompted by memories and stories left over from their distant childhoods, occasionally crept cautiously up to the manse and left some small offering—a woven scarf, perhaps, or a basket of apples or eggs—in the hope that such a gesture might attract good luck. Mornan, however, disdained all attempts to placate him and never so much as acknowledged the gifts. It seemed he had withdrawn entirely from the world, and the world in its turn left him well alone.

It was only an hour short of midnight when Anyr reined in his sweating horse at the manse gates. No lamps burned in any of the windows, and under the moon's cold light the manse had a gloomy, threatening air that might have daunted the hardiest of souls: Anyr, however, didn't hesitate but sprang down from the saddle and approached the gate. There was no bellrope, but when he pushed the gate it swung back with a creak of rusted iron and admitted him to the overgrown garden. There was a path of sorts, though it was hard to find and follow among the tangle of neglected shrubbery, and Anyr set off toward the house, ignoring his horse's nervous whinny as it lost sight of him in the darkness.

As he approached the front door he felt his pulse, already over-rapid, quicken still further until it was almost physically painful. Deep down he knew he was afraid both of this house and of its strange inhabitant, but he was determined not to allow the fear to overtake him. Think of Sivorne, he told himself sternly. Mornan is the one man who can help her. And he is just a man, not a demon or a god.

The door, like the gate, had no bell, but there was a heavy iron ring set into the ancient wood, though clearly it hadn't been used for many years for it was all but rusted into place. At last Anyr wrested it free, and knocked three times. The sound, shockingly loud against the night's silence, boomed eerily through the house. There was no response. After perhaps a minute, Anyr tried again. Still nothing—or did he glimpse, just for a moment, the flicker of what might be candlelight through one of the windows? Quickly he moved to look, peering through the glass; but the window was so grimy that it was impossible to see anything beyond it, and the brief glimmer of light had vanished. Sighing, and wondering whether Mornan was asleep, away, or simply ignoring the summons, Anyr turned toward the door again—and jumped back with a cry of shock as he came face to face a motionless figure which had materialized noiselessly and with stunning swiftness from the dark.

Granite-hard eyes glittered in the moonlight under brows like mountain overhangs. A deep voice said, "What do you want?" and Anyr knew that he was confronting Mornan in person. Hastily collecting his wits, he made a formal bow. "Sir, I apologize for disturbing you at such an hour—"

He didn't get any further. Mornan snapped,

"Uninvited visitors are a disturbance at any hour. I ask again: what do you want?"

His height, Anyr thought; that was the most extraordinary thing about him. Mornan must have been over six feet tall, and his stature was emphasized by the fact that he was shockingly gaunt. He looked more like a walking skeleton than a living man, and for a moment Anyr was utterly discomposed. Wishing fervently that he had some light to show the sorcerer more clearly and dispel the unnerving effect of his silhouette, he struggled to find the words to explain his mission.

"Sir," he began, "I am Anyr, son of Lord Aronin of Caris, and I am in desperate need of your help!"

He couldn't see Mornan's expression, but he felt his immediate reaction like a physical change in the air.

"I help no one," the sorcerer said curtly. "Go to your witches and your priests and ask their aid."

"They have tried to aid us, sir, but they've failed," Anyr persisted. "This is a matter over which only true sorcery can prevail! Please—you *must* help me!"

"*Must?*" Mornan repeated the word with faintly mocking amusement, and Anyr thought he saw—or rather, sensed—the ghost of a smile. "That is not a word to which I have ever taken kindly. I am not interested in your troubles, I am not interested in you, and I will thank you now

121

to go away and leave me in peace. Good night to you."

He started to turn away, but stopped as he heard the rattle of steel. Slowly he looked back and saw that Anyr had drawn his sword.

"Young man," the sorcerer said drily, "I would strongly advise you to put away your blade and not even think of trying to coerce me. I've no particular wish to hurt you, but I will not tolerate threats."

"I don't care what you will or won't tolerate," Anyr said with the defiance of desperation. "I've come for your help, and I won't leave here until you promise to give it." He hefted the sword: "I admit I only have physical weapons to back me, but I'm not afraid to match them against your powers if I have to."

Mornan hesitated. "You're *that* desperate?" The faint deprecating humor was back in his voice, and Anyr flushed.

"Yes, I'm that desperate. Desperate enough to risk my life and soul if that's my only hope of moving you. I've nothing to lose."

"Can anything be so important that you'd jeopardize your own existence for its sake?" Mornan asked.

Anyr held his gaze, forcing himself not to be disconcerted by the chill glitter which was all he could see of the sorcerer's eyes. His voice shook and he said: "This can. This is." Then suddenly the pain within him wouldn't be held back any longer but had to have an outlet. His self-control collapsed and he burst out, "Damn you, are you completely devoid of feelings? Are you a man, or a shade? There's no one else I can turn to, but you won't even hear my story! Gods, what can I do but plead with you—if you've any humanity at all, *help me!*"

He thought at first that he'd shown fatal weakness, that Mornan would either laugh in his face and walk away or speak a contemptuous curse that would reduce him to a quivering ruin. But instead the sorcerer paused again—and when he finally spoke, although his tone was brusque there was no hint of mockery.

"Well," he said. "I suppose I must commend your passion and your dedication to your cause, even if you're a fool in other ways. Any humanity, you say . . ." He uttered a short, sharp laugh. "Very well, young man: I'll hear your story." The glint of his eyes became keener. "You may have five minutes of my time."

Anyr stared at him, astonished by such a sudden and unexpected change of heart. "You mean—" he began in confusion.

Mornan interrupted him. "Take it or leave it, it's of no account to me. Five minutes; no more." And he added pointedly, "You'll find my sense of time is uncannily accurate."

Anyr's mind whirled as he struggled to adjust to the twists and turns of Mornan's attitude toward him. He didn't understand the sorcerer's logic, if indeed logic played any part in his reasoning. But one thought stood out clearly. There was a chance—one chance, one only—that he might succeed in winning this strange recluse to his cause where others' pleas over the years had failed to move him. Strangely and inexplicably, the thought gave him new courage, and suddenly he found the words he needed coming easily and eloquently to his tongue as he began to unfold his tale. He told Mornan of Sivorne's conviction that some malevolent spirit was following her, and then of how Ghysla had stolen Sivorne away and attempted to take her place, only to be unmasked and to reveal herself as the same creature who for the past three years had befriended him in the guises of animals and birds. Mornan listened without interrupting and with an impassive demeanor that offered neither hope nor discouragement until, as Anyr explained how his father had driven Ghysla into the windowless tower, he abruptly reached out and laid a hand on the young man's arm, making him jump.

"One moment," he said sharply. "The creature is a shape-shifter, you say? Describe her true appearance again, more carefully."

As best he could, Anyr recounted how Ghysla had looked when she had finally lost her grip on her shape-changing powers and reverted to her true self. When he finished, Mornan nodded.

"And she was afraid of fire?"

"Yes. That's how the men trapped her; she didn't dare come near our torches. Then, when she was locked in the tower, we lit bonfires all around the house and called in the wise-women.

They tried to cast a binding spell, but it didn't work. All the creature did was start screaming."

"Screaming?"

Anyr shifted uncomfortably at the memory of Ghysla's awful cries. "It was a horrible sound—unearthly, devilish. I think the witches' spells might have hurt her, but they couldn't control her." He hunched his shoulders. "I can't hate her for what she's done. In fact, in a way I pity her."

"Pity her?" Mornan looked at him speculatively.

"Yes. It's terrible to witness any creature in such torment, and the worst of it is, she really believes that she loves me as woman loves man. It's insane, of course—she isn't even human, though I don't truly know what manner of being she is—but I think she truly does believe it, and that's what drove her to commit this crime. She doesn't understand that—"

"No," Mornan said emphatically. "No more."

Anyr blinked and looked up. "No more?" he echoed in consternation. "I don't understand."

"I mean that I've heard enough. Wait here. I'll be but a few moments."

Anyr didn't have a chance to protest before the old sorcerer had pushed open the door of the manse and disappeared into the black interior. Baffled, he could do nothing but wait as instructed until, after perhaps two minutes, Mornan reappeared. By the grey moonlight Anyr could see that the sorcerer had cast a long cloak about his shoulders and was carrying a small leather bag.

"Well?" Mornan demanded as Anyr stared at him. "What are you waiting for? Let's be on our way at once."

Anyr's mind groped toward comprehension. "You mean you'll help me?"

"Yes, I'll help you. No, don't start asking questions; I've better things to do than waste time explaining my reasons. I'll help, and there's an end to it. Do you have a horse at the gate?"

Anyr nodded. "If you'd care to ride—"

"I've never had need of a horse in my life, and I don't intend to change the habit at my age. You ride; I'll have no trouble keeping up. Come, now. I assume this mission is urgent?"

Anyr swallowed back the host of questions that were clamoring to be answered, and only said, "Yes. Yes, sir. And . . . thank you."

"Thank me if I restore your bride to you unharmed," Mornan replied curtly. "Until and unless I achieve that, you might as well save your breath."

And before Anyr could respond, he strode away toward the gate.

CHAPTER IX

Mornan didn't speak a single word on the journey back to Caris. Once or twice Anyr addressed him but the sorcerer didn't reply, and by the time the house on the clifftop with its flickering circle of bonfires came in view, Anyr was feeling thoroughly ill at ease.

They went in through the gates, and almost at once Aronin saw them and hastened forward.

"Anyr!" Then he stopped as he saw the sorcerer. For a moment his face registered astonishment, then he recovered himself and bowed courteously.

"Sir, I can't begin to express my gratitude for your—"

"Put those fires out," Mornan said, completely ignoring Aronin's attempt at a greeting. "And tell the women to stop chanting. It's perfectly obvious they're achieving nothing, so they'll oblige us all by ceasing that caterwaul."

Anyr looked apologetically at his father, and Aronin, with a snort of indignation, strode away to do the sorcerer's bidding. Mornan watched from a distance as, one by one, the fires were doused, then when the last flames had died he stalked toward the throng gathered round the house, Anyr hurrying to keep up with him. Word of his arrival had already got about, and he was greeted by a silent, uneasy crowd. They drew back at his approach as though he were an alien species, and watched him wide-eyed as he stopped at last and looked up at the tower where Ghysla was trapped.

There was no howling coming from the tower now. When the witches fell silent, so Ghysla, too, had ceased her cries as she was released from the pain their spells had caused her. Mornan stared for a long time at the windowless turret's black bulk, stark against the starry sky, and Anyr, standing beside him, had the unnerving feeling that the old man was seeing straight through the solid stone wall into the room beyond. Behind him Aronin and Raerche hovered, but no one had the courage to speak until at last the sorcerer let his gaze fall and turned around.

"Show me your great hall," he said.

Quickly, before anyone else could speak, Anyr volunteered, adding, "I'll fetch a lamp."

"If you need one, very well." Mornan sounded irritated, and quickly, half afraid that he might change his mercurial mind even now, Anyr commandeered a lantern from a nearby group of people. He would have liked to speak to his father and Raerche, to explain something of his story, but Mornan gave him no chance. He set off toward the main door, his cloak billowing behind him, and Anyr was forced to run after him without time to say a word to anyone.

He caught up with the sorcerer in the entrance hall. The house was eerily quiet; the doors to the main hall stood open, and as they approached, the lantern's light illuminated the wreckage within. Mornan stopped on the threshold, gazed about at the scene and said, "Her work?"

"Yes."

"Mm. She has a temper on her, it would seem." He moved into the hall, taking care to avoid the debris on the floor, and stopped in the room's exact center. Anyr started to follow, but the sorcerer held out a forbidding hand.

"No. I don't need you, and I don't want you to stay. Rejoin the others, and stop anyone else from entering the house. I wish to work alone."

"But, sir, you don't know the way to the turret."

"I don't need to. Go now, and don't argue with me."

Disappointed, but aware that persistence wouldn't achieve anything, Anyr retreated back to the door. He was about to leave when he remembered the lantern, and he held it up.

"Sir, you'll need light—"

"I will not."

Anyr let his arm fall back to his side. He was just about to step through the doors when memory jogged him again and he remembered the other thing, the vital thing, and he called out again.

"Should I fetch you the key to the turret door?"

The sorcerer's voice echoed in the hall's emptiness. "I've no more use for keys than I have for lanterns. Go away, young man. *Go away!*"

Anyr, feeling chastened and angry and fearful and hopelessly confused, ran back to join the waiting crowd outside.

Something had entered the house. With her cat-like senses Ghysla felt the intrusion of a new presence, and knew immediately that here was a source of power far greater than the witches'. But what was its nature? *What?*

Suddenly, she was afraid. More afraid than she had been of the women's chanting and the pain it had brought flaring into her head; more afraid than she was of the bonfires, or of the torches that burned outside her prison door. She turned and twisted about in the dark, her thin arms hugging her narrow body, and her wild hair flew from side to side like whips as she tried to escape from the sensation that was growing within her.

But she couldn't escape from it. Someone had entered the house of Caris where others had not dared, and that someone was stronger by far than she was. She whimpered, then dropped to a crouch on the floor, her huge eyes wide as she tried to see through the pitch darkness. But the intruder, whoever he was, wasn't climbing the spiral stairs toward her, but was somewhere below her. *Below her*—she sprang up again and skittered to the farthest corner of the turret room, grazing her elbows on the rough stone as she tried to back away out of reach of the power she felt focusing almost directly beneath her feet.

The effort availed her nothing. She could still feel the presence down below; indeed, it was growing stronger by the moment. Tears welled in her eyes, spilling down her cheeks and splashing on to the now torn and grubby bodice of the wedding gown as fear swelled to terror. What would happen to her now? What was this newcomer capable of, and what would he do? She didn't want to be hurt; she couldn't bear any more pain such as the witches' spells had inflicted. Oh, gods, she thought in miserable desperation, pity me, and help me!

But she knew her appeal was in vain. The old gods were lost and gone. They had died out with her own people; they couldn't return to aid her now. Softly, hopelessly, Ghysla fell to her knees again on the cold stone floor, and wept.

Below in the great hall, Mornan stood with head bowed and arms crossed on his breast. The bag he had brought from the manse lay beside him, but he had no need of it. He could feel the fluttering, frightened mind of the creature he had come to do battle with, and his heart was pounding suffocatingly in his chest; not through fear or through excitement, but with another and deeper-rooted emotion.

At last, he raised his head. Unlike most sorcerers he had little truck with ceremony and ritual; he had never needed wands and incenses and magic sigils, and in the past had only used them because ignorant laymen—whom he held in the deepest contempt—expected to be impressed by some miraculous show. Now, with no one to observe him, he could dispense with paraphernalia. The unencumbered power of his mind was enough.

He stared up through the ceiling, through the floor above, up the twisting spiral of the turret stairs. On another plane, inaccessible to others, he saw the two torches which Aronin had left burning outside the door of Ghysla's prison. A thin, hard and humorless smile crossed his face briefly; he made a pass in the air with one hand and quietly uttered an alien word. At the top of the windowless tower the torches flickered, guttered, and went out, plunging the stairwell into darkness. Mornan smiled again, then his eyes closed and he began to concentrate harder. He reached out for the creature within the turret room, felt his power curl around her, gripping her mind, holding her, compelling her to do his bidding. From high above his head a terrible scream rang out, a cry of panic, of pleading, of agony. *No, no, no*—Mercilessly, Mornan tightened his hold on her, knowing now that, demon though she might be, she was no match for him.

At the top of the darkened stairway, there was a sudden, loud *click* as, with no key to move them, the tumblers of the doorlock turned over. Slowly, very slowly, the door started to swing open. And Ghysla, whimpering now, clutching her scalp and tearing at her hair as she fought against the compelling force which assailed her, heard echoing through her mind like a clap of thunder the sorcerer's implacable voice.

I COMMAND YOU—COME TO ME!

Her feet were moving of their own accord. She couldn't stop them, couldn't fight the pull that dragged her against her will toward the door and the stairs beyond. She tried to grip the lintels as she was propelled out of the room, but a burst of power snatched her clawing fingers away and sent her staggering down the first spiral.

"No!" she protested. "No, no, *please*, don't hurt me, don't—" Something unseen pushed the small of her back and she stumbled down a dozen more steps, almost losing balance and measuring her length. She could see the end of the flight and the passage beyond, and now it was as though invisible hands had grasped her arms and were pulling her willy-nilly with the strength of a dozen horses. Along the passage she ran helplessly, then went sliding and bumping down the main stairs, grabbing vainly at the banisters as they sped by but unable to catch hold of them. Before her now was the door to the great hall, and she knew, *knew* that her tormenter was in there. A terrific force flung her at the door, and she pressed against it, scratching feebly at the wood with her long nails. She couldn't speak coherently; all she could do was mumble an agonized plea—*oh, stop, please stop, take the pain away, I'm so frightened*—

Suddenly, the agony in her mind vanished. At the same moment the power released its hold on her, and she sagged like a rag doll, sucking air into her lungs with a groan of relief. Then a voice—not in her head this time, but real, physical—spoke from the other side of the door.

"I won't hurt you, unless you try to disobey me. Enter the hall. Let me see at last what manner of creature I am dealing with."

Very gently, Ghysla pushed at the door. It swung slowly open and she peered cautiously around its edge. To her surprise she saw that there was only one solitary figure in the hall beyond. She stared at him. He was so *tall*—taller than any human she had ever seen. And he was old. His long hair was white, with only a few streaks of iron grey where some pigment stubbornly remained, and his frame was as gaunt as a scarecrow's, his cheeks hollow, his eyes deepsocketed, his lips once full and generous but now shrunken to a thin, hard line. But his eyes weren't an old man's eyes. They burned with vigor and alertness, like vivid topaz jewels—and they were focused with shrewd intensity on the shadows where she lurked.

"Enter," he said. Ghysla couldn't disobey, but even as she moved forward she felt a tiny flare of defiance within her. If she must show herself to this sorcerer, then she would show herself not as Ghysla—who would surely be as unlovely to his eyes as she had been to Anyr's—but as the image of Sivorne, whom she had tried to hard to become. Just once, she thought, just one last time, she would be beautiful again.

She slipped through the door and shuffled into the hall. She couldn't bring herself to look at Mornan's face but advanced slowly and uncertainly, until at last her nerve failed her altogether and she stopped ten paces from where he stood.

Mornan gazed at her. What he saw was a young and lovely golden-haired girl, but he knew that her appearance was a sham. What, he wondered, lay beneath the mask?

He spoke sternly. "So, creature. What do you mean by causing such trouble to the good people of this house?"

At last Ghysla found the courage to look up at him. 'I didn't mean to," she whispered. "Please . . . you must believe that I didn't mean to harm anyone!" Her eyes filled with misery then as she realized how useless her words were, but she couldn't stop herself from finishing: "I love him so much. . . ."

"Love?" Mornan repeated. "Who is it that you love?"

"A-Anyr." Ghysla sniffed and rubbed her eyes with a clenched fist.

The sorcerer gazed around him at the wrecked

hall. "And all this," he said, "all this wanton destruction—this was for the sake of love, was it?"

Tears were glittering on her lashes now. "He scorned me ... I thought he loved me ... Oh, but he did, he *did!* He *told* me so! When I was the seal, when I was the deer—he said he loved me then! But then he turned on me, and he said he loves *her* instead! He thinks I'm evil—but I'm not evil, I'm not, I'm *not!*"

Mornan's eyebrows knitted together over the crags of his brows. "You stole away a young man's true bride, and tried to win him for yourself by trickery. Isn't that an evil deed?"

"No! I didn't mean—"

"Any harm. So you say. But you have *done* harm, haven't you? Great harm."

A pause; then Ghysla hung her head. "It was because I love him so much. I thought he was being forced to marry her." Her shoulders began to shake as tears trickled down her cheeks. "I thought he wanted *me* to be his bride ... I've loved him for so long, and he loved me, he *said* so, but I'd never dared to let him see me as I really am, and then, when I heard that he was to wed—" And suddenly she was babbling, blurting out the whole of her dismal story from the very beginning. She confessed everything to him, every thought, every act; and as the words spilled from her lips Mornan stood listening and watching her in silence.

Finally the flow ceased. Ghysla looked miserably at the sorcerer, and Mornan spoke at last.

"So: You feared to let Anyr see you as you truly are, but you believed he loved you and not Sivorne. So you did all this because you thought it would make him happy?"

Ghysla nodded again. "Y-yes . . ."

"But now you know the truth, don't you? You know you were grievously mistaken." He sighed heavily. "Oh, you pitiful, foolish child . . . There's no point in pretending any longer, or in maintaining your charade. Cast off your mask. Show me your true self."

She looked up him fearfully. "No . . . please, I don't want to—"

"You must," Mornan said, his tone immovable. "I command it."

She couldn't fight him. She had already experienced his power, and she was helpless against it. So she closed her eyes, and the mask of Sivorne's image slid away from her so that she stood scrawny, ugly, lank-haired and owl-eyed before the sorcerer. The wedding gown no longer fitted her but hung in ridiculous folds about her thin frame. Sivorne's dainty shoes slipped from her feet, which were too unhuman and misshapen to be contained by them. The crumpled veil and chaplet made a grotesque and almost comic finishing touch, and Ghysla—the real Ghysla—covered her face with her clawed hands and wept bitterly for her own shame and grief.

Mornan said quietly: "What is your name, child?"

He had seen the truth, she thought. Why

137

should he not know all the truth? It could make no difference.

She whispered: "My name is Ghysla."

There was a long silence. Then, in a gentle and almost wistful voice, Mornan said: "Ah. Ghryszmyxychtys."

Her head came up sharply and her eyes widened until they seemed to fill her face, her mouth a small, round "O" of shock. A hiss escaped her and transformed into words. "You speak—" then her voice failed her.

"Yes," said Mornan. "I speak the elder-tongue. The language of your own race."

"But that's impossible! My people are all dead. I am the last, and there's no one else left who knows the old tongue! No one but me!"

"Ah, little dark one, you are wrong." She realized that Mornan's own eyes were changing, growing larger; his face, too, was altering, subtly but surely, becoming narrower and bonier still. "There is one other." One hand, the fingernails suddenly elongated, touched his own breast lightly. "I have been called Mornan now for more years than I care to remember. But before I resolved to speak only the language of humans, my name was Myrrzynohoenhaxn—and that was the name my mother gave to me."

Ghysla gasped. She couldn't believe what she was hearing—yet at the same time she only needed to look at the sorcerer's face to know that it was true. This was no trick to win her confidence. He was too powerful to need such devices. He *was* of her own race ...

"Little Ghysla," Mornan said, and there was kindness and compassion in his voice. "I understand perhaps better than most what drove you to do what you have done here. You see, many, many years ago—long before you came into this world—there was another of your kind who, like you, fell in love with a human man. In those far off days humans didn't hate or fear the fey folk, but respected them, perhaps because rather than in spite of their differences, and the two races coexisted in peace. So her story was happier than yours, for the man she loved came to love her too, and they were wed in the fashion of her people." He smiled sadly. "I was their one and only child."

Ghysla only continued to stare at him with her huge, shocked eyes. At length Mornan continued.

"My father, being human, came to the end of his natural span in just a short while by our reckoning. He died four hundred years ago. My mother might have lived on for many more centuries before her time, too, was done, but her grief at his death was such that she chose instead to follow him to the world that awaits us all beyond this life. I never thought to see another of her race again. I thought I was the last to carry the old blood. It seems I was wrong."

Ghysla blinked. A small, muffled sound escaped her, and a new tear fell like a diamond on to the floor. Mornan laughed softly, though not unkindly. "Why are you weeping? Surely not for me!"

"I d . . . I don't know . . ." But she did know. She *was* crying for him; and for herself, too. Crying for the old, lost ages, for her long-dead kin, for the love Mornan's mother had known and which she herself had believed, for a short and wonderful time, that she too might know. And, though a part of her didn't want to admit it, she was crying for Anyr and Sivorne.

"Did you kill his bride, Ghysla?" Mornan asked softly. "Or does she still live?"

"She . . . still lives."

The sorcerer exhaled a soft breath. "Yes," he said. "I thought so. Where is she?" Ghysla didn't reply, and after a few moments he added: "You must tell me, my child. You know that, don't you? It's the only way to right the wrong you have done."

Feeling as though she were dying inside, Ghysla said. "There is a cave in the mountains, near Kelda's Horns. She is there. I . . . cast a spell on her."

Mornan frowned. "What spell?"

A long hesitation. Then Ghysla whispered: "The Sleep of Stone."

"Oh, gods." Mornan closed his eyes. "Ghysla— Ghysla, do you realize what you've done? Don't you know that there's only one way in which that spell can be reversed?"

Ghysla frowned. She hadn't thought about

how the spell might be broken, for the idea of bringing Sivorne back from limbo had never been a part of her plan. Mornan had opened his eyes again and was looking intently at her. To her surprise and dismay she saw deep sympathy in his expression.

"You don't know, do you?" he said unhappily.

Aware that her heart was beginning to beat too quickly, Ghysla shook her head. Mornan stared down at the floor.

"The Sleep of Stone," he told her hollowly, "is one of the most formidable enchantments ever known to our people. In the old days, our elders decreed that it must be used only in the direst emergency. There was good reason for that edict, Ghysla—for the Sleep of Stone can only be broken if the one who cast the spell should willingly take the place of their victim. If Sivorne is to be woken, then you must enter the limbo world in her stead. It's the only thing that can be done to save her."

Ghysla stared at him in dawning horror. Then, shocking them both, a new voice, shaking with passion, spoke out from the far end of the hall.

"No! No—there must be another way!"

CHAPTER X

Mornan whirled around. Framed in the hall entrance, his frame rigid and his eyes burning with emotion, was Anyr.

"*What is this?*" the sorcerer demanded. "How long have you been standing there?"

"Long enough to have heard what you said to her."

"I told you not to disturb me!"

Anyr squared his shoulders defiantly. "You are not master of this house, Mornan the sorcerer. I have the right to be here." He walked toward them, undaunted by Mornan's furious glare, and as he approached, Ghysla suddenly burst again into violent tears. He was here, her beloved, her adored one; and his presence awoke a fresh wave of grief within her heart.

Mornan glanced at her but didn't address her. Instead he looked at Anyr, who had stopped before them and was staring at Ghysla. "There is no other way, Anyr. Believe me, if there were, I would use it."

Anyr continued to look at the sobbing Ghysla

for a few moments longer, then abruptly met the sorcerer's gaze. "Oh, gods, what am I to do? I don't hate her, Mornan, you know that: I pity her! But pity isn't love. I love Sivorne, and no one could ever take her place. If it's true that she's still alive and could be restored to me, then I—I want her back. I want it more than anything else in the world!" He reached out and clasped the sorcerer's arm. "Nothing else matters to me. You understand that, don't you, Mornan? Tell me, please—what am I to do?"

"There is nothing you can do," Mornan told him gravely. "Only Ghysla can choose whether or not to release Sivorne. I could compel her to do it; I have the power to bind her to my will; but I won't do that, and I don't believe you would want me to. The decision must be hers alone."

There was silence. Ghysla, with a great effort, had stemmed her tears and now stood motionless, her face hidden by the hair that fell like a tangled curtain over her face. At last Anyr turned to her.

"Ghysla . . ." Her name didn't come easily to his lips. "Mornan is right; no one can justly force you to bring my Sivorne back to me. I can't condone what you did and I can't admire you for it; but I believe that you were driven by love and not by evil intent as I first thought. I blame myself in many ways. I understand now why you believed that I loved you and not her, and I'm sorry that you must suffer because your love isn't reciprocated. But I don't love you, Ghysla, not in that way, and I never could. It's different, don't you see? My feelings for the creatures you became, the seal and the deer and the bird, are another kind of emotion altogether. They're a fondness, an affection, but they're not truly love." He stared down at the floor, shaking his head sadly. "Perhaps we humans use words too freely, but then to us one word can have many different meanings. For me ... well, what I feel for Sivorne is *real* love, and nothing can change that. I want only her, and without her my life will mean nothing."

Hesitantly, Ghysla raised her eyes to look at him. "As my life will mean nothing without you," she whispered.

"Yes," Anyr's expression was grave. "I realize that. But I can't change my feelings, any more than I can change the course of the sun across the sky." He hesitated. "I can't demand that you sacrifice yourself to give her back to me; I haven't the right. Nor will I plead with you to do it out of love for me. That would be dishonorable. But you were ready to go to any lengths to try to win me, so you know as well as I do how deep love can run, and the lengths to which it can drive those of us in its throes. Therefore when I tell you that Sivorne is all that matters to me, and that I'd die for her or kill for her, I think you understand those feelings." Another pause. "I couldn't ever love you, Ghysla; and if, as Mornan says, there really is no other way to restore Sivorne to me, then my dearest hope is that you'll be willing to exchange your life for hers. I'm sorry if that's cruel, but it's the truth and I see no point in hiding it. So I can only hope and pray that that is the choice you will make."

Ghysla turned her head away. She couldn't answer him, not immediately, not like this. Anyr stepped back, and as he drew level with Mornan the sorcerer spoke in an undertone and with a faint trace of irony, "That was a handsome speech."

Anyr flashed him a quick, resentful look. "It was no such thing. I simply felt it better to be honest."

"Cruel to be kind?"

Anyr flushed. "No! Not intentionally." He regarded the older man with angry eyes. "Perhaps you don't comprehend the feelings that drive me."

"Perhaps I don't." The sorcerer glanced over his shoulder to where Ghysla stood, a silent, solitary figure with her head bowed. "But she does. You can be sure of that."

Anyr's anger crumbled and he nodded. "I know. That's the worst of it. After all, I'm responsible for her plight, aren't I? If it hadn't been for me, she'd never have been brought to this."

Mornan sighed. "She brought herself to this, Anyr: Even I with my biases and my much-vaunted conscience have to acknowledge that. I only wish there was another way to resolve it."

Anyr's eyes glimmered with pain. "You are *sure* that there's no other way, Mornan? Perhaps some forgotten magic which might break this spell without hurt to anyone?"

"No." Mornan shook his head. "I wish it were otherwise, but no. She must decide."

Ghysla, meanwhile, stood deep in thought and oblivious to the two men's quiet exchange. As Mornan had said, as Anyr had said, the terrible choice was hers alone to make. She could laugh in their faces and declare that she would never be persuaded to repeal the spell. She would lose her love, but then he was already lost to her: at least Sivorne couldn't have him either, and she herself would keep her life and her freedom.

But then on the heels of defiance came despair. She had lost Anyr. That was the nub of it, the worm at the heart of the bud. Whatever she did, however long she might live, he would never be hers. It wasn't a choice between herself and Sivorne: There *was* no choice for Anyr. What had he said? "*Without her, my life will mean nothing.*" And she had answered him: "*As my life will mean nothing without you.*" It was true: true for them both. Could she love Anyr and yet condemn him to spend all his remaining years grieving for Sivorne? She knew what grief could do to a tormented soul. She couldn't sentence Anyr to that. She *couldn't*.

She raised her eyes, looking through the veil of her hair to where Mornan and Anyr stood. They were silent now, waiting for her to speak, waiting for her decision. Anyr's future lay in her hands. Oh, but she loved him. She thought of the years ahead of her, the decades, the centuries of loneliness, burdened by the yoke of Anyr's misery where she had longed in vain for his love. She didn't want that. She didn't want to live without him.

Slowly, Ghysla raised her head. Anyr saw the movement and his body tensed. He longed to speak, but Mornan touched his arm warningly and with a great effort he held his tongue. Ghysla looked at them both, the young man she adored, the old man who was half of her own kind. Her tongue touched her lips, moistening them. She was afraid—deeply afraid—but she had made her decision and wouldn't go back on it now.

She said, very quietly, "I will do it, Anyr. I will give her back to you."

Anyr exhaled sharply and covered his face with his hands. Mornan gazed at Ghysla with a mingling of sorrow, regret, and admiration. "You are sure, my child?" he asked gently.

"Yes. I am sure." Her eyes, burning, focused on Anyr's motionless figure. "I've nothing to live for now."

Anyr looked up and met her gaze intensely. He didn't have the words to express his gratitude; they wouldn't form, they wouldn't come. Bereft, there was only one way in which he could show her a little of his feelings, and he moved toward her, caught hold of her hands and, raising them to his lips, kissed them.

"Thank you, Ghysla!" he whispered, his voice choked with emotion. *"Thank you!"*

There was uproar when Anyr and Mornan emerged from the house with Ghysla walking between them. A group of men, with Aronin and Raerche in the forefront, saw the fey little creature and surged toward her, their voices rising in a hubbub of furious accusation. Before they could reach the trio, however, Mornan held up a hand sternly.

"Enough! There will be no retribution!"

Their awe of him gave him authority, and the babble of voices died down. Mornan raked the company with a fierce glare and continued: "The bride is alive and unharmed. We go now to fetch her, and this child will go with us and help us to right the wrong she has done, and which she now repents."

Someone shouted from the back of the crowd. "Repentance isn't enough, sorcerer! We want her punished!"

"Punished?" With chilling accuracy Mornan pinpointed the man who had called out, and fixed him with a searing, contemptuous look. "Put away your righteous indignation, fellow! The child will suffer more than enough in other ways without your petty reprisals—let that knowledge content you!" Dismissing the man, he turned to Ghysla. "Come, little one. No one will hurt you now."

They moved through the press of people, who drew back to make way. No orders were given, but Mornan knew that there would be no attempt to follow them. In a small, sad procession they made their way to the gates; the sorcerer first, Ghysla after him, and Anyr trailing a few paces behind. As they emerged on to the deserted road, Mornan looked back at the young man and said, "It will be a long and weary walk, and what lies at its end may not be pleasant. Stay here if you wish to."

"No." Anyr shook his head. "I'll come with you, if you'll permit it."

"As you wish." Mornan said no more, and they walked on.

It was a strange, almost dreamlike journey. The streets of the harbor town were empty of life and silent as an untenanted tomb; not even the shadow of a cat moved in the stillness. The moon hung low above the sea, casting a thin, eerie pall over the nightscape, and when they left the town behind for the high moors the wind came gusting and dancing to meet them, snatching at cloaks and hair, soughing and singing to them in its unearthly voice.

They walked on in silence toward the mountains. Ghysla was leading now; no one spoke. The moon set, casting a silver path across the sea from the west as she sank below the horizon, and the night became utterly dark but for a scattering of starlight. They reached the mountain foothills, the crags rising higher and higher around them. Looking up and ahead Anyr could see the twin peaks of Kelda's Horns looming like the skull of some nightmarish giant before them. He shivered, but said nothing.

The path began to rise, and soon they were climbing over rough scree and up ever steepening gulleys. Here in the crags they were sheltered from the wind, and the silence was acute and chilling. At last, Ghysla stopped. She looked up at Mornan, then pointed to a dark cleft in the rocks ahead.

"There," she said.

Mornan straightened, a gaunt silhouette against the stars, and looked up to the sky. Eastward a pearly grey glimmer touched the horizon, and the sorcerer spoke quietly to Anyr.

"It's almost dawn. Come; this isn't a deed that should be done in kindly daylight."

They moved toward the cave entrance. Ghysla went in first, hesitating only a moment before she ducked through the low gap. Following, Anyr and Mornan found themselves in pitch blackness; Anyr gave an involuntary gasp, but the sorcerer raised one hand, murmured something the younger man didn't catch, and a pale, cold sphere of blue light sprang into being overhead. Ghysla looked up fearfully, and Mornan smiled.

"His eyes are less able than ours to see in darkness, child," he said. "Don't fear it—it isn't fire. Now: Show me where Sivorne rests."

The glowing sphere drifted above them as Ghysla led them across the cave's uneven floor. Nearing the shelf which once had been her own bed she stopped, and wordlessly pointed.

At first, Anyr didn't realize what he was looking at. He saw the shape on the shelf and thought it simply an abnormality of the rock, a quirky seam of pale minerals running through the darker strata. But as he drew closer the abnormality abruptly resolved into something else—and with a strangled shout he stumbled back, clapping a hand to his mouth to stop himself from retching as he recognized the gruesome, petrified figure of Sivorne.

As Anyr staggered away, Ghysla too stared down at the statue. She was not shocked—she alone of all of them had known what to expect—but the still, graven image, so lifelike yet so remote and chill, struck a different kind of horror into her heart. This was *her* handiwork. And now she must face the reality of her own fate; the knowledge that she must undo the spell she had wrought, and embrace the ice-cold living death of petrification in her turn.

She turned her head and looked at Anyr. He was standing near the cave mouth and had recovered his composure enough to force himself to look at Sivorne again, though from a distance. His face was blank, frozen, and only his eyes, burning with pain and yet with resolution, gave away the turmoil of emotions within him. And something within Ghysla died. Until this moment she had been harboring a last, gossamer-thin thread of hope that there might be a reprieve, that at the final instant Anyr would turn to her and rekindle her dream. But now she saw the depth of her folly, and with a soft, despairing cry she turned, reaching out blindly, seeking comfort though none was to be found.

Hands gripped her arms, a presence moved before her, and Ghysla hid her face in Mornan's cloak as the sorcerer drew her into a powerful embrace. She wanted to cry but she couldn't, the tears wouldn't come, as if she were already turning to stone. In a tiny, shuddering voice, she whispered, *"I'm so afraid . . . "*

"I know, little one. I know." His eyes were over-bright when at last she looked up at him, and she wanted to cling to him, beg him to help her, to turn back time, to make the world all right again.

But there was nothing he could do. To ask it would be futile and unfair, for even Mornan the sorcerer, her half-kin, didn't have so much power. She stepped away from him, her clawed fingers clenching one last time in the fabric of his cloak before she released her grip, and she turned to face the stone ledge and what it contained.

"Tell me what I must do," she said.

Mornan told her. It was a simple spell, foolishly simple, and she felt a crazed desire to laugh as she memorized the words she must say and the actions she must perform. As she began to speak, the sorcerer withdrew to stand beside Anyr, who wanted to look away but found himself compelled by something beyond his control to watch. As before, when she had cast the binding spell, strange and ephemeral shapes began to materialize about Ghysla's lonely figure, and Anyr thought—though for the rest of his life he could never be sure, and never quite recapture the memory—that he heard a sound from far, far off, like spectral, inhuman voices singing a poignant and eldritch song.

On the stone shelf, a shuddering ripple ran through the recumbent statue. A faint flush of color tinged the marble cheeks, and the dull sandstone hair was suddenly shot through with gold. A single tress lifted, blowing across Sivorne's deathly white forehead. The skirt of her white lawn nightgown moved by the smallest fraction. And the sound of a long, slow exhalation murmured through the caves as Sivorne's stone lips became flesh, parted, and she began to breathe.

Ghysla's chant ceased on an odd, soft discord. Her upraised arms fell to her sides and she cast her gaze down. Anyr gave a cry, and ran forward.

"Sivorne! Sivorne, oh, my Sivorne!" He fell to his knees beside the ledge, repeating her name over and over again as he gathered her into his arms. Her eyelids fluttered; a spasm went through her as the last traces of the enchantment fled, and her blue eyes opened, regarding him filmily.

"Anyr . . . ?" Sivorne sounded drowsy, half lost in a dream. "Wh . . . what are you doing here? Where are we?"

Anyr opened his mouth to explain, but before he could speak Mornan intervened. "No, Anyr, don't try to tell her yet. She's weak, and she may suffer shock if we don't take the greatest of care. Let her rest." And he held a hand toward Sivorne's face, the index and middle fingers extended. "Sivorne."

She saw him for the first time, and a frown crossed her face. "Who are you?"

The sorcerer didn't answer her question but only smiled reassuringly and said: "Sleep, Sivorne. Sleep for a little while longer."

The frown smoothed away and Sivorne's lovely eyes closed. She began to breathe lightly but evenly in the steady rhythm of peaceful relaxation. Anyr gazed hungrily at her face for a few moments, stroking her hair gently, then at last looked up at Mornan.

"We must return to Caris!" His whole demeanor had changed utterly; misery and despair were gone, and in their place was a joy too great to contain, yet too great to express in anything as limited as mere words. "We must take her home, and broadcast the happy news!"

Mornan sighed. "Yes, Anyr. Take your bride home. There is nothing more to be done here."

A small sound, so faint that had his senses been less acute he might have missed it altogether, suddenly impinged on Anyr's ears. He tensed, and watching the rapid change of expression on his face, Mornan realized that in the happiness of his reunion with Sivorne, Anyr had utterly forgotten the presence of Ghysla. The sorcerer himself had not forgotten, not for one moment, but at the instant of Sivorne's release from the spell his courage had failed him: he had averted his eyes from Ghysla, and since then had been unable to bring himself to look at her again. Now though, he steeled himself, and both he and Anyr turned their heads.

Ghysla stood where she had stood throughout the speaking of the spell, and she was watching them. Mornan felt as though a cold, tight web had enfolded and constricted his heart, for in all the centuries of his inhumanly long life he had never seen such longing, such sorrow, and such helplessness in the eyes of any living being. Ghysla's feet could no longer move. She was rooted to the floor of the cave, and her thin legs had already become one with the rock, sculptured stalagmites that merged eerily and terribly with her still living body. Her hands moved like trapped birds, frightened, uncertain; the dull glitter of granite was already beginning to thread through her hair.

Anyr whispered: "Oh, gods . . ."

"It's too late to call on them now," Mornan said softly. "Besides, her gods are dead and they cannot hear you."

"Can . . ." Anyr swallowed. "Can *she* still hear me . . . ?"

"Yes. It isn't yet complete."

Ghysla's lips were moving. They looked deformed now as the enchantment which had passed from Sivorne's body to hers took a greater hold. Crystal shimmered in her mouth; her hands had stopped moving and were taking on the soft shine of marble. Only her enormous, owllike eyes were unchanged.

Suddenly Anyr moved toward her. He reached out to touch her shoulders, and felt the remote smoothness of stone beneath his fingers. Every instinct in him screamed at him to flinch back; he fought the urge, conquered it, gazed into her slowly changing face.

"*I'm sorry.*" Oh, but the words were so worthless, he thought, so futile; they could mean nothing to her now. But he had to say them. He had to grant her that much, before it was too late. "Ghysla, I can't ask you to forgive me; I can't expect that of you. But ... I owed you everything, for you gave Sivorne back to me of your own free will. And I'll never, *never* forget that."

Though it was faint, he felt a shiver of some unnameable emotion go through her, communicating itself even through the stone of her body. On an impulse which he couldn't and didn't want to resist, he reached to his own throat where, on a slender chain about his neck, hung a silver locket. The locket had been his mother's, and Anyr treasured it. He couldn't help Ghysla now; but this small and precious token, he thought, might help to convey in however small a way the gratitude which his words could never hope to express.

He fastened the slim chain about Ghysla's neck, so that the locket lay on her breast, which now had taken on the soft glow of marble. Anyr gazed at it for a few moments, then leaned forward and kissed Ghysla gently on the mouth. He felt no urge to flinch this time: It was a deliberate kiss, gentle; not the kiss of a lover but the sincere gesture of a friend.

Ghysla's consciousness was drifting away toward the quiet, dark void of limbo, but enough awareness still remained for her to feel the kiss and understand its meaning. With a great effort she moved her lips one last time. Her voice was almost inaudible, but Anyr was just able to make out her final, poignant words.

Ghysla whispered: *"I shall always love you. . . ."*

CHAPTER XI

If he lived for a hundred years, Anyr knew he would never forget his last sight of Ghysla. He wrapped the sleeping Sivorne in his cloak, and as he carried her out of the cave and emerged into the cool, pale glory of a perfect dawn, he had looked back, just once, and the image he had seen was imprinted forever on his memory. Ghysla, a thing of stone now, stood in the center of the cave. Her head was turned toward the sunrise, and the fingers of her hands curled protectively over Anyr's silver locket, hiding it from view as she clutched it close to her. She had the air of a young faun startled from a safe haven, and the expression on her marble face was one of faint puzzlement, yet with something else underlying it, something that Anyr believed—and he hoped, he prayed he was right—was akin to peace.

Mornan followed him slowly out of the cave. The sorcerer hadn't spoken for some time and didn't utter a word now, but his eyes and Anyr's met and, reading the silent message in Mornan's look, Anyr turned away and began to carry Sivorne carefully down the steep path, leaving the old man alone.

When Anyr was out of earshot, Mornan faced the cave entrance once more. The statue that had been Ghysla regarded him solemnly, and for what might have been one minute or ten Mornan held her gaze before, in a voice charged with emotion, he said softly:

"Goodbye, little one. Perhaps one day, and in another time beyond the reach of this age of humans, we may meet again."

The glowing blue sphere he had conjured, and which still hovered above Ghysla's head, winked out, and the cave sank into deep gloom. Mornan gazed at the narrow entrance, beyond which the sad little statue could no longer be seen. Then he raised one hand and drew a sigil in the air before him, at the same time speaking five soft, secret syllables in the tongue of the old folk, his mother's people, Ghysla's race.

The silvery sound of water impinged on the silence, and from a small cleft in the rocks above the ledge a tiny stream sprang into being, cascading down the rock face and reflecting the rising sun in a rainbow of shimmering colors. Mornan watched the fall, watched as it formed a small pool beside the cave entrance—a pool that would never overflow; that, too, was a part of the magic—and smiled a sad and private smile. Ghysla had been so afraid of fire. Water then, fire's opposite and inimical to it, was a fitting choice for his own small memorial to her. The laws of this land said that no man might disturb the ground where a spring had its source, and so this place would now be safe from desecration. Whatever else might befall over the centuries to come, Ghysla would at least rest undisturbed.

"Ghryszmyxychtys," Mornan said gently. "Be at peace, little dark one. Be at peace."

His face devoid of all expression, he turned away and walked down the path. He found Anyr waiting for him in the shelter of a bluff that overlooked the vast panorama of the coastline and the sea beyond. Sivorne slept on beside him, and at the sorcerer's approach the young man sprang to his feet, a question in his eyes and on his lips. Mornan forestalled him with a gesture, giving him a sad, weary smile.

"There's nothing more to be done, Anyr. Take your bride home, and rejoice."

Anyr gathered Sivorne into his arms once more. He paused to kiss her brow tenderly, then, hugging her tightly to him, he began to walk away. Mornan followed them at a distance. He had seen the look in Anyr's eyes as he kissed the sleeping girl, and knew that, however deeply he himself might grieve over her fate, Ghysla's choice had been just and right. Her day, the day of her kindred—his kindred, too, he reminded himself—was done, and the future belonged to humankind: the Anyrs and Sivornes of this world. For him, the sun was setting; for them it was rising on a new age. And surely it was only right that they should be allowed to face their dawn unhampered by those whose race was run.

The great vista of the sea before him blurred suddenly, and Mornan felt tears trickle down his cheeks and splash on to his cloak. Weeping. By all the ancient gods, how many years had it been since he had last wept? An old fool's indulgence, he thought with self-disparagement; then pushed the thought away. Why should he not weep, if he was moved to? There was no one else to cry for Ghysla. Surely that was justification enough for his tears.

He was lifting a hand to brush the moisture from his lashes when Anyr, now some fifteen paces ahead of him, turned and looked back. For a moment Mornan was shamed by the knowledge that the young man had witnessed his moment of weakness: but then he saw the answering telltale glitter in Anyr's own eyes, and knew that his were not the only tears to be shed for Ghysla today.

Anyr's lips curved in a hesitant smile. He waited for Mornan to draw level with him, then said, "I'll keep your secret, Mornan, if you'll keep mine."

Mornan's answering smile was a little grim but there was a hint of comradeship in it. "A fair bargain."

A pause. Then Anyr said: "Will you come back to Caris with us? I know you want no reward for what you've done, but . . . I'd like you to come. If you're willing."

Mornan was about to refuse politely but firmly, but suddenly a small inner voice said: Why not go with them? For so long now he'd scorned any company but his own, clinging proudly to his mother's heritage and thinking that human society had nothing to offer him. Yet didn't his father's blood run as strongly in his veins as his mother's did? Over the years he'd ignored and all but forgotten the human side of the legacy his long-dead parents had left him. Perhaps now the time had come to remember it again, and to renew the old ties.

The vista before him blurred again. Impatiently Mornan brushed at his eyes, then coughed to hide a sudden constriction in his throat.

"Thank you, Anyr," he said. "I'll come with you, and gladly."

He could hear the sea now. Its vast, elemental voice mingled with the ceaseless whistle of the wind, and together under the rising sun they seemed to be singing an unimaginably ancient song which transcended time and made no distinction between the old and the new, the past and the present and the future. An eternal song, Mornan thought, eternal as the world itself. Today it was an elegy to the passing of Ghysla's people; doubtless one day in the future it would lament the end of the human race, too. But not for a long time, a very long time yet. And that was as it should be.

Once he had been Myrrzynohoenhaxn; but

that name no longer had a place here. It was time to lay it to rest in the fondly remembered but vanished past, where it belonged. He was Mornan now, and would be simply Mornan through the peace of his remaining years.

Mornan raised his face to the bright morning and felt the sun's strengthening warmth like a balm in his heart as, with his two companions going before him, he walked on down the mountainside toward Caris.

CODA

He had thought it before and now he thought it again; she *was* such a lovely girl. And now, as he reached the end of his tale and fell silent, the old man's heart was touched in a way he couldn't express as he saw, highlighted by the sun, the glint of tears in her blue eyes.

"Child, forgive me," He smiled a slow, sad smile. "The last thing I wanted was to make you weep!"

She shook her head. "No—no, Grandfather, please don't blame yourself. I'm just being foolish; I—" She sniffed long and loud, and the young man held out a red kerchief for her to dab at her eyes.

"I've never heard such a sad story," she said after a few moments, when she'd regained her composure. "That poor little creature—to suffer such a dreadful fate!"

The old man's faded eyes grew thoughtful. "Was it so very dreadful? I sometimes wonder."

"What do you mean?"

Stiffly, using his carved stick, the old man rose

to his feet. "Come," he said. "Come with me." He began moving toward the grotto, and when they hesitated he raised a gnarled hand and beckoned. "It's all right. I simply wish to show you something."

Still a little uncertain but curious nonetheless, the young couple followed him across the rough ground to the cave. All three stepped inside, and the old man stood for some moments gazing at the fantastic rock sculpture within.

"Look carefully, now," he said at last, "and tell me what you *really* see."

There was silence for a minute or two. Then the red-haired youth's voice echoed softly in the cave. "It looks like . . . no. No, it's just the sunlight. It must be."

The old man turned a quizzical gaze on the girl. "What do you think he sees, child? What do you think he sees but doesn't quite dare to acknowledge?"

"I . . ." Then she bit her lip. "I don't know . . ."

"But I think you do. I think your hearts are telling you the truth. Look again, both of you, and don't fear to admit what you believe."

The young man's face was haggard, and tears began to trickle from the girl's eyes once more as she wrung her unsteady hands together in a nervous movement.

"It looks . . . oh, Grandfather . . . I can see a face! A sad, strange little face . . ."

Yes, he thought: They had realized it now. The erosion of centuries had worn the stone's more delicate contours away, but in certain lights and to unclouded eyes the contours of the small, sharp features were still just visible. Those great eyes, haunted by memories which others had long forgotten. The thin cheeks, the pointed chin, both less and yet more than human. And the wide mouth which might—just might—have been curving in the hesitant ghost of a smile.

The couple were gazing at him, waiting for him to speak. The old man nodded gravely. "Yes," he said. "This is Ghysla."

The girl exhaled a soft, awed sigh. "Then the legend is true . . . ?"

"Oh, yes. Ghysla has been long forgotten, but she existed, and her story happened just as I have told it."

The young man moved tentatively toward the statue and bent to gaze at what had been Ghysla's hands. No one could recognize them now, for the fine marble was worn down, worn smooth, the delicate detail of the clawed little fingers lost beyond recall. After a few moments the young man spoke.

"There's a glint of something silver . . ." He straightened, his eyes shining with wonder. "The locket. Anyr's locket. Grandfather, it's still here— after all this time, she still holds it!"

"Indeed she does." The old man smiled, and the youth turned suddenly to his betrothed.

"When this year of my apprenticeship is complete, my master has promised that I shall be allowed to work in silver. I shall fashion such a locket for you, and it will be as beautiful as Ghysla's! It will be our own talisman!" The girl blushed with delight, and he turned to the old man once more. "Would that not be fitting, Grandfather?"

"It would be very fitting, my son. It is, after all, the symbol of a very great and enduring love. I'm sure that Ghysla herself would have been pleased by your compliment to her."

By unspoken but instinctive agreement, the three of them moved back toward the cave entrance. On the threshold, the girl lingered for a moment, looking back at the silent and motionless stone figure.

"It seems so sad that she must stay forever in darkness," she said wistfully. "I wonder if she misses the warmth of the sun, and longs to feel it again?"

"No," the old man replied, "I don't believe that she does. She was a creature of the night more than the day. Besides, how can we begin to guess what manner of worlds are inhabited by one who sleeps the Sleep of Stone? Perhaps, in her dreams, the sun and the moon both shine for her still."

They stepped out into the bright day. "We'll take our leave of you, Grandfather," the young man said, touching his brow respectfully. "Thank you for telling us the story of this place. We'll both remember it for as long as we live."

"Yes, thank you, Grandfather," the girl agreed. Then, shyly, she added: "Our wedding is in one month from this day. We're to be married at the harborside, by the fisherman's priest. Would you—that is, if you would do us the honor—" She faltered.

"You are very kind, my child, and I thank you for the compliment of your invitation," the old man said. "But I think that your wedding will be a celebration better suited to the young, so I will decline. But I wish you both long life and fruitful happiness. Farewell."

They smiled—then the girl, on impulse, darted forward and stood on tiptoe to kiss the old man's leathery cheek. "Bless you, Grandfather!" Her betrothed had already begun to move away toward the downward path; she started after him, then paused. "I didn't ask you your name. Please tell me—then at least if you won't come to our nuptials, I can send you a cut of the wedding cake!"

He chuckled. "Well, that's a generous thought. My name?" Slowly, perhaps even wistfully, a smile spread over his wrinkled features. "My name is Myrrzynohoenhaxn."

She stared at him. Her eyes were wide but though her mouth opened, no sound emerged. So, he thought; she had listened to his story with the greatest care, and the significance of the name had not escaped her. She understood now. He saw it in her eyes. She understood.

With a great effort, the girl collected her wits. Then, in an old-fashioned gesture that the old man had not seen for more than two centuries, she dropped him a deep, reverential curtsey, before she turned and ran away down the path after her betrothed.

After the young couple had gone, the old man stood motionless for a very long time. What, he wondered, had made him break with the rule he had imposed upon himself so long ago? It had been decades—no, he corrected, it had been *centuries*—since he had spoken his own true name to himself, let alone to another soul, yet for some reason which he couldn't fathom he had *wanted* to tell that pretty, innocent, flaxen-haired girl who he really was. Foolish of him, and vain, but he had wanted her to know.

He put a hand up to his cheek, his fingers touching the place where her lips had brushed his skin. Perhaps that was what had motivated him; her kiss. Spontaneous, generous, as though he truly were her grandfather and not just an old man whom she was polite enough to address by a courteous title. He knew now who she reminded him of. He'd known all along really, his memory hadn't failed him; but had been reluctant to admit it even to himself. Sivorne. Sweet, golden-haired Sivorne, who had married Anyr of Caris and had lived happily with him for half a century in the great house on the clifftop overlooking the town. Their bones had long turned to dust, but their descendants lived and ruled there still, though Mornan had lost count of the generations now. So many years, he mused. So many long years stretching away into the past, down the endless road of his memory. He had been thinking about that a great deal recently; thinking about the centuries that lay behind him and asking himself if, perhaps, he was growing tired of his life. He was old—unimaginably old by human standards; and though in the terms of his mother's race his time might have many years more yet to run, he *felt* old. And lonely; so lonely. In Anyr's day he had enjoyed a brief respite from his solitary existence; he had been persuaded to mingle in human society, emerge from his shell, cast off some of his self-imposed reserve, and he had been happy. But the happiness hadn't lasted, for the new friends he had made during those years had all passed away, and with their dwindling he had begun to withdraw once more, until again he had become a recluse, a hermit, just an old man with whom no one passed the time of day. Those two young people, he realized, so happy on the threshold of their life together, were the first human souls with whom he had so much as spoken in more than twenty years.

He looked over his shoulder at the entrance to the grotto, then, leaning on his carved stick, moved slowly toward it. Fine spray from the waterfall brushed his face like tears; through the mist it made, Mornan smiled, then stepped over the threshold.

It only took a little imagination and he could see her clearly. Not eroded stone as she was now, worn to a faint and all but shapeless ghost, but in her own half-human and delicate form. He could see her ragged hair again, see her thin arms, her clawed hands, her huge eyes that were like windows to her soul. Very gently, he reached out and touched her, feeling the cold—strange, how it was always, *always* cold—of her marble face.

"Ah, Ghysla; little Ghysla." Even his voice sounded old he thought, creating dry, whispering echoes in the cave. "Maybe yours was the wiser choice after all. Our day was already done, little dark one, even before you first set eyes on your beloved Anyr. It has been too long, Ghysla. It has been far too long."

How many times had he stood in this spot and spoken to Ghysla as though she were still alive and could hear him? A foolish old man's fancy, it was. She wasn't here, not really. She was gone, like all the others of her kind and his. He was alone. Truly, he was alone.

The knowledge of what he would do came like a gentle summer sunrise, slowly and calmly and with utter certainty. What had he told himself, all those years ago, when he stood in this very place with Anyr of Caris? That the future belonged to humankind, and that they should be allowed to face their dawn unhampered by those whose race was run. It was true. And he had delayed the inevitable for long enough. He knew why he had come here now. He knew what he wanted to do.

Strangely, as he withdrew his hand from Ghysla's stone face and laid it against his own breast, he felt no trepidation; only a faint sense of curiosity. He let the carved stick fall. Someone would find it, and it had years of good use in it yet. His other hand closed over the first, close to his heart, and he closed his eyes.

Such a simple spell. Poor Ghysla had memorized it easily, and now, as he began to whisper the words in the old, lost language of her kind, Mornan felt, as she had done, the presence of spectral, ephemeral forms gathering in the cave, gathering about him as though to welcome him. From somewhere came a strange, unearthly singing, alien yet so beautiful that he could have wept. Mornan wanted to sway in rhythm to their lovely song, but he resisted the impulse, standing still and straight as an oak tree beside Ghysla as the last words of the spell were uttered and echoed quietly away.

Ah yes; he could feel it beginning. Numbness, like sleep creeping over him. His feet and legs were cold—but the cold was far from unpleasant. That surprised him; he had anticipated discomfort, pain, even fear, and he was no more immune to those things than any wholly human man; but this ... it was, he realized, quite delightful. The sweet singing was growing louder and he couldn't tell whether it was simply in his mind or if the owners of those beautiful voices were here with him, in the cave, calling to him, summoning him ...

Something like the lightest of zephyr breezes

touched his face, and the clove scent of gillyflowers filled the grotto. Beside him, something moved. He could still open his eyes, though the feeling was gone from his limbs and torso now, and he did so. No: He had imagined it. Ghysla hadn't reached out to touch him.

DAW

Jennifer Roberson

THE NOVELS OF TIGER AND DEL

Tiger and Del, he a Sword-Dancer of the South, she of the North, each a master of secret sword-magic. Together, they would challenge wizards' spells and other deadly traps on a perilous quest of honor.

☐ SWORD-DANCER	UE2376—$4.99
☐ SWORD-SINGER	UE2295—$4.50
☐ SWORD-MAKER	UE2379—$5.99
☐ SWORD-BREAKER	UE2476—$4.99

CHRONICLES OF THE CHEYSULI

This superb fantasy series about a race of warriors gifted with the ability to assume animal shapes at will presents the Cheysuli, fated to answer the call of magic in their blood, fulfilling an ancient prophecy which could spell salvation or ruin.

☐ SHAPECHANGERS: Book 1	UE2140—$3.99
☐ THE SONG OF HOMANA: Book 2	UE2317—$4.99
☐ LEGACY OF THE SWORD: Book 3	UE2316—$4.99
☐ TRACK OF THE WHITE WOLF: Book 4	UE2193—$4.99
☐ A PRIDE OF PRINCES: Book 5	UE2261—$4.99
☐ DAUGHTER OF THE LION: Book 6	UE2324—$3.95
☐ FLIGHT OF THE RAVEN: Book 7	UE2422—$4.99
☐ A TAPESTRY OF LIONS: Book 8	UE2524—$5.99

DAW

Tad Williams

Memory, Sorrow and Thorn

THE DRAGONBONE CHAIR: Book 1
☐ **Hardcover Edition**   0-8099-003-3—$19.50
☐ **Paperback Edition**   UE2384—$5.99

A war fueled by the dark powers of sorcery is about to engulf the long-peaceful land of Osten Ard—as the Storm King, undead ruler of the elvishlike Sithi, seeks to regain his lost realm through a pact with one of human royal blood. And to Simon, a former castle scullion, will go the task of spearheading the quest that offers the only hope of salvation . . . a quest that will see him fleeing and facing enemies straight out of a legend-maker's worst nightmares!

STONE OF FAREWELL: Book 2
☐ **Hardcover Edition**   UE2435—$21.95
☐ **Paperback Edition**   UE2480—$5.99

As the dark magic and dread minions of the undead Sithi ruler spread their seemingly undefeatable evil across the land, the tattered remnants of a once-proud human army flee in search of a last sanctuary and rallying point, and the last survivors of the League of the Scroll seek to fulfill missions which will take them from the fallen citadels of humans to the secret heartland of the Sithi.

—and coming in March 1993—

TO GREEN ANGEL TOWER: Book 3
☐ **Hardcover Edition**   UE2521—$25.00

In this concluding volume of the best-selling trilogy, the forces of Prince Josua march toward their final confrontation with the dread minions of the undead Storm King, while Simon, Miriamele, and Binabek embark on a desperate mission into evil's stronghold.

Buy them at your local bookstore or use this convenient coupon for ordering.

PENGUIN USA   P.O. Box 999, Bergenfield, New Jersey 07621

Please send me the DAW BOOKS I have checked above, for which I am enclosing $_____ (please add $2.00 per order to cover postage and handling. Send check or money order (no cash or C.O.D.'s) or charge by Mastercard or Visa (with a $15.00 minimum.) Prices and numbers are subject to change without notice.

Card #_____ Exp. Date _____
Signature_____
Name_____
Address_____
City _____ State _____ Zip _____

For faster service when ordering by credit card call **1-800-253-6476**

Please allow a minimum of 4 to 6 weeks for delivery.

DAW
Tanya Huff

VICTORY NELSON, INVESTIGATOR:
Otherworldly Crimes A Specialty

☐ **BLOOD PRICE: Book 1**   UE2471—$3.99
Can one ex-policewoman and a vampire defeat the magic-spawned evil which is devastating Toronto?

☐ **BLOOD TRAIL: Book 2**   UE2502—$4.50
Someone was out to exterminate Canada's most endangered species—the werewolf.

☐ **BLOOD LINES: Book 3**   UE2530—$4.99
Long-imprisoned by the magic of Egypt's gods, an ancient force of evil is about to be loosed on an unsuspecting Toronto.

THE NOVELS OF CRYSTAL
When an evil wizard attempts world domination, the Elder Gods must intervene!

☐ **CHILD OF THE GROVE: Book 1**   UE2432—$3.95
☐ **THE LAST WIZARD: Book 2**   UE2331—$3.95

OTHER NOVELS

☐ **THE FIRE'S STONE**   UE2445—$3.95
Thief, swordsman and wizardess—drawn together by a quest not of their own choosing, would they find their true destinies in a fight against spells, swords and betrayal?

Buy them at your local bookstore or use this convenient coupon for ordering.

PENGUIN USA P.O. Box 999, Bergenfield, New Jersey 07621

Please send me the DAW BOOKS I have checked above, for which I am enclosing
$_____ (please add $2.00 per order to cover postage and handling. Send check or money order (no cash or C.O.D.'s) or charge by Mastercard or Visa (with a $15.00 minimum.) Prices and numbers are subject to change without notice.

Card #_____ Exp. Date _____
Signature_____
Name_____
Address_____
City _____ State _____ Zip _____

For faster service when ordering by credit card call **1-800-253-6476**

Please allow a minimum of 4 to 6 weeks for delivery.